ALSO BY

LIA LEVI

The Jewish Husband

TONIGHT
IS ALREADY
TOMORROW

Lia Levi

TONIGHT
IS ALREADY
TOMORROW

*Translated from the Italian
by Clarissa Botsford*

Europa
editions

Europa Editions
1 Penn Plaza, Suite 6282
New York, N.Y. 10019
www.europaeditions.com
info@europaeditions.com

Translation by Clarissa Botsford
Original title: *Questa sera è già domani*
Translation copyright © 2021 by Europa Editions

The author thanks Gaia Panfiliand Adelia Battista for their affectionate
and skilful support while writing this book.

Library of Congress Cataloging in Publication Data is available
ISBN 978-1-60945-649-8

Lia Levi
Tonight Is Already Tomorrow

Book design by Emanuele Ragnisco
www.mekkanografici.com

Prepress by Grafica Punto Print – Rome

Printed and bound in Great Britain by Clays Ltd, Elcograf S.p.A.

That sacred Closet when you sweep—
Entitled "Memory"—
Select a reverential Broom—
And do it silently.

'Twill be a Labor of surprise—
Besides identity
Of other interlocutors
A probability—

August the Dust of the Domain—
Unchallenged—let it lie—
You cannot supersede itself
But it can silence you—

—EMILY DICKINSON (1273)

TONIGHT
IS ALREADY
TOMORROW

CHAPTER 1

The young Mrs. Rimon had approached him fleetingly as they were leaving the synagogue, and had asked him for a private meeting. "I'd like to bring my son to you," she'd said hurriedly, under her breath. Rabbi Bonfiglioli had been a little surprised. He seemed to remember that the boy was just a kid, certainly not old enough to be preparing for his bar mitzvah. In any case, the Rimons were nothing special. They were a good family, but they were not particularly observant; tepid at best. Sure, they came to services en masse for the obligatory festivals—Rosh Hashanah and Yom Kippur— always with a motley gang of relatives in tow, but that was it. He had seen the mother there on her own every now and again, always in a newly tailored dress, but she looked more like a polite spectator than a woman of fervent faith. There was one thing that had caught the rabbi's interest, however: the prayer book she clutched in her hand. The print looked ancient, and the cloth binding with big floral patterns on it was well worn. He would have paid anything to be able to take a look at it, but he didn't know the woman well enough to ask. "I wonder whether she'll bring it when she comes to the appointment?" He only allowed himself to indulge in frivolous thoughts of this kind on the Sabbath.

The boy was more or less as he remembered: a bright-looking child who was not even remotely intimidated by the heavy furniture that made his office so oppressive. Imagine, the rabbi himself sometimes had to step out of that room in order to lift his spirits a little; even if only to dive into the corridor.

Without waiting to be invited, the boy sat himself down in a low chair next to his mother. The gesture was entirely natural, without a hint of arrogance. It was as if he were already conscious of the fact that—wherever he was in the world—there would always be a place for him.

"What's your name, and what grade are you in?" That was the script, and Rabbi Samuele Bonfiglioli was not about to alter it.

His name was Alessandro. He only used his full name; he didn't like nicknames and neither did anyone else in his family. He was eight years old, and this coming October he would be going into Fifth Grade.

The rabbi was bewildered, again. The script was not right.

"Fifth Grade at eight?" he asked.

"Yes, but I turn nine in February." The boy seemed apologetic. "I'm two years ahead," he murmured quietly, almost inaudibly.

"Good lad," Rabbi Bonfiglioli answered mechanically, while his thoughts were beginning to wander.

Why had he been asked to meet the child? He remembered something he had heard through the grapevine about a Jewish boy—a little genius—who had skipped a couple of grades in public school because he'd already learned everything on his own.

What does a rabbi have to do with educational acrobatics of this kind?

He had better things to do. His task in life was to study the Torah and pass his knowledge on to the next generation. Getting boys ready for their bar mitzvah was his calling. When his eyes chanced upon a pupil's expectant gaze, the joy made his heart miss a beat.

There was a long silence. The boy rocked in his chair and

then got up to observe the furnishings and objects in the room. It was as if he were taking ownership of them. The rabbi could see that his curiosity had been fired by the heavy brass paperweight on his desk, a globe held up by four muscular figures, which was actually an inkwell filled with black ink. He was, indeed, fascinated. He wondered whether the powerful figures might be Cyclopes but then decided that, given they were in a rabbi's home, they had to be replicas of Samson.

"Rabbi, Sir." Emilia Rimon was hesitantly trying to start a conversation. "I asked for an appointment because I needed to ask you a question." Her son, the boy in front of him, had announced a few days earlier that he only believed in God sometimes. "This seems like quite a serious matter for a Jew, don't you think?" she added hastily.

Rabbi Bonfiglioli wasn't at all keen to answer. The woman's fumbling attempt to reel him in had not been effective. She didn't look like a woman who was overflowing with religious zeal. Apart from anything, she hadn't even brought the prayer book he had been so interested in. Her tentative question felt like a pretext she had hurriedly pulled out of thin air. The vague impression that he had had on their first encounter must have been correct, after all.

Emilia Rimon was simply driven by an irrepressible urge to show off this child prodigy: a boy who was so intelligent that he had become the family's pride and joy. Somehow, though, the idea that the legend of this brilliant kid might somehow have already reached the ear of the Chief Rabbi of the entire Genoa community tormented him.

Was he supposed to answer the woman's spurious query? The rabbi was an uncomplicated kind of person, a teacher who loved the Torah. Nothing more. The kind of maxims some of those "wonder rabbis" might come out with—false prophets and preachers all—were simply not his thing. He was one for straight talk, and preferred those humble words which had been handed down since the beginning of time. Soon, however, before he was even aware of it, he felt his irritation dissolve into a wave of indulgence. This was the way it always went. Human weakness ended up moving him.

"Good boy," he said, in a tone of voice that was so bland it could have been used in any number of situations. "I understand that you like learning. It will soon be time for you to study the Torah."

Then he bent over the boy and whispered in his ear, "You say you only believe in God sometimes. You should know, though, that God believes in you always."

Alessandro hadn't wanted to go to the rabbi; it was his mother who had dragged him there against his will. Now, however, he had to confess, that phrase the old man had spoken into his ear struck him as beautiful.

Perhaps even true.

It felt as though Marc had been lurking behind the front door waiting for them. He opened it wide before his wife had time to put her key in the lock.

"You took Alessandro to the rabbi? Why would you do that?" he asked, as soon as they came in. He had had no idea; it was Nonno Luigi who had told him.

"Well," Emilia improvised, "I realized the rabbi had never met our son. Alessandro never comes to synagogue with me on the Sabbath."

"That's because he's at school on the Sabbath!" Marc shouted, no longer bothering to hide his irritation. Then he stopped suddenly, turned on his heels, and strode out of the house setting off for the laboratory. His wife was always so harsh with him; there was really no need to stoke the flames.

CHAPTER 2

That evening, Emilia sat through dinner hardly saying a word. She answered anyone who dared ask her a question in monosyllables. The only time she came to life was when they discussed the kitchen window that wasn't closing properly. For days, there had been a loud crack like a gunshot every time the shutters slammed shut in the wind, because the wood was weather-worn. They needed to get a move on and repair it soon.

Luigi was used to his daughter's frequent long silences, and he didn't find them pleasant. He had lived in this house since his wife had died. Eight years had gone by, and he couldn't remember any laughter ringing down the hallway. Unless it was with his grandson.

Alessandro was different. There were times when he couldn't get to the end of a sentence because a word cast a spell on him. In a stuttering display of affection, he would turn it around in his hands as if it were a precious gem, completely dumbstruck. Then he would suddenly burst out laughing, and everyone else would follow suit, although they were baffled by his behavior.

"What did Rabbi Bonfiglioli say?" Luigi asked his grandson, who was busy picking the peas out of his soup one by one and didn't answer right away. Then the boy told him about the inkwell in the shape of a globe with the Samsons holding it up on their shoulders. He wanted to return his grandfather's effort to make conversation without giving away anything else. When dinner was over, he set his chair down next to the old man. He loved his tall, solitary grandfather. When they went out together, he thought he looked like one of the trees lining their street. Nonetheless, he wanted to keep what had taken place at the rabbi's house to himself.

Luigi understood. All of a sudden, he turned around and asked his son-in-law, "What time is Osvaldo coming?"

Marc had been quiet throughout dinner, too.

"Soon, I think," he answered sullenly.

"Well, I'll go and get ready then." Luigi set off, putting on a brave show of speed and vigor. He knew they were following him with their gazes, and didn't want to be seen as a shuffling old dullard.

Osvaldo was his other son-in-law, his daughter Wanda's husband. His daughters had both found excellent husbands—one better than the other—but they didn't seem very happy about it. Who knows what they were thinking, those girls. It wasn't as if either of them was God's gift to men.

When Osvaldo arrived, Luigi and Marc were ready for him, waiting in the hall. Wanda wasn't there. When the husbands went out with their father-in-law, she usually came over and spent the evening chatting with her sister.

"She must have something better to do," Emilia said to herself, although she knew it wasn't true. They had argued the night before. A petty fight. Since he had been widowed, their father had always lived at her place, and Wanda seemed to take this for granted. Emilia would have liked some recognition from her sister, at least a "thank you" every so often, but Wanda had answered rudely. Emilia had insisted on having him, claiming that the old man and his grandson would keep each other company. Wanda should have understood that sometimes words are merely a mark of generosity and kindness. The fact was, Wanda thought she was superior. She certainly wasn't more beautiful; her eyebrows were so straight, they made her expression stony, like an Ancient Roman statue. She was more elegant, perhaps. Being elegant and receiving invitations was easy: all you had to do was spend money.

Thinking about it, she wasn't put out one bit that her sister hadn't come over that evening. The men had gone out, she could hear Cesarina doing the dishes in the distance, her son was in bed, and she was on her own in the quiet, gray rooms. She read a book. She worked on a knitted sweater for the boy. Knowing she didn't have to finish either of these tasks, *that she didn't have to*, gave her a huge sense of freedom.

The men, father and sons-in-law, always had the same table in the *osteria*. The bottle of red wine and the pack of cards were the same every time, too. The gilded brass lamp hanging from the middle of the ceiling, with a long, bendy arm like a pelican's neck, shed an oblique ray of light on them: friendly, concentrated, but not too bright. They played a slow game, their heads down, each of them feeling as if they could be anywhere in the world, at any time in history, with no obligation to belong to any context in particular. They went home early. At the front door, Marc stood to one side as usual, biding his time politely and absent-mindedly. He let his father-in-law go ahead and turn the key in the lock with a certain importance.

In his bedroom that evening, Luigi opened the window so that he could smoke a cigar without bothering anyone. The sea was not visible, but knowing that he would see it at the end of the road if he went out was enough for him. Imagining the sea and seeing it was one and the same thing for him: it was his personal victory over time and space. And age, perhaps.

There were no stars. The only light was the moving tip of his lit cigar. He swirled it in the air to cheer himself up. He smiled.

Was it possible that he loved his sons-in-law more than his

own daughters? They had been his little girls, after all! He had taken them to the beach on his shoulders, one on each side, just like he did today with his grandson. How can things change so much? He felt he had nothing in common with the women they had become. He simply tried to stay as far away as possible from their prickly characters, their denial of joy.

The following day, he took his grandson by the hand and led him to the port at Foce to watch a new ship being launched. On their way home they didn't talk, but they were happy.

When Alessandro was younger, Luigi used to tell him the same stories over and over, alongside bits and pieces from the Bible. His wife Rachele had been the one who knew all the Jewish stuff, and over the years of their life together she would often tease him: "You're a Jew but you know next to nothing of the Torah!" But her tone was always indulgent. She didn't have her daughters' bad temperament. After Rachele's death, Luigi felt it was his duty to pass all those little stories on to his grandson, but he could never quite remember all the details. He would get the characters mixed up (all except Moses, that is), or he would make a protagonist of a folk tale a Jew, so that Robin Hood would end up being Judas Maccabeus' side-kick. His grandson didn't know any difference, and even if his daughter Emilia happened to be listening in, she wouldn't notice.

But it was something else that tied Alessandro to his grandmother: a gold chain and pendant she had left him in her will. The pendant was beautiful, its indented border hiding tiny Hebrew letters in its curves. The centerpiece was what caught the eye, though: the Star of David had been inlaid in a different color of gold, making it stand out. Luigi decided to gift it to Alessandro right there and then, given that his mother had so foolishly decided to take him to see the rabbi. He handed over the trinket and explained that King David had placed the six-pointed star on his shield, and that was why it had become the symbol of Judaism. He didn't add any other details, because he was afraid of slipping up. His wife had never felt more present to him than in that moment, checking up on his every word.

Alessandro was confused by how much he liked both the pendant and the story. He took the chain and pendant and put it in his drawer inside a shell he had picked up on the beach. His grandfather decided to build him a little chest made of blue cardboard, with a knob on the drawer, telling him it would be like a secret baby drawer tucked inside the real drawer. Especially in the early days, Alessandro opened and shut the tiny drawer continuously. He loved weighing the delicate chain with the Star of David pendant in his hands. He would turn it in different directions to see how the colors changed in the sunlight. He would close his fist over it until it hurt, then put it back, only to feign gleeful surprise on discovering that the little drawer concealed something in its tiny belly. Finally, he would put the necklace to bed as carefully as if it were a newborn baby.

"A pendant should always be on your person, around your neck," his mother would say, but Alessandro always answered, "I prefer it this way. Having it to myself to look at is much better than letting other people see it." Spectacles are the only things that are completely useless if you don't put them on your eyes, he once said, thinking out loud. His mother couldn't think of anything to say because, as she reflected, she had never seen anyone sitting and gazing at a pair of spectacles. A few months later, Alessandro started to claim that he remembered his grandmother giving him the Star of David. She had handed it over with such tenderness, he insisted, even though Rachele had died before Alessandro had turned one. After a while, this imaginary memory became the imaginary memory of the whole family.

CHAPTER 3

Emilia had not taken long to understand that she didn't love her husband and never would. Their marriage had been arranged, but that wasn't the reason. It was the way things worked in the Jewish community, and it didn't make much difference whether you met your future husband strolling in the street or a well-meaning relative had introduced you. Her friend Ines had married a man who laughed all the time because he was an idiot. Ines said he was a man of good character. Emilia and her sister had adopted the term "good character," joking about it every time they came across someone stupid.

Marc was different, though. He was Belgian by birth, his family had moved to Holland, he held a British passport and his mother tongue was French. He was the epitome of the healthy progress Jews had made in every corner of an increasingly liberal modernized Europe. Emilia didn't have any interest in the complexity of Jewish destiny, however. It was enough that she had married a Jew in order to show respect to her family. The fact that he was foreign—even though he had settled in Genoa many years before—bothered her somewhat. It made her feel different from the rest of the community, although nobody could tell he was an outsider when he spoke. What does it take to learn Italian, after all, for people who already speak many languages? It's the easiest language of all. He sounded completely Italian when he spoke, and his writing was practically perfect. He even managed to throw in some Genoese dialect every now and again. What weighed on Emilia was that her husband wasn't able to introduce a single relative, which was frowned upon in their community. There was one advantage, though: no parents-in-law or acquired siblings underfoot.

Marc went to see his mother in the Netherlands occasionally, but once they all three had to go because she had wanted to meet her only grandchild. The first thing they did on arrival was rent a Dutch outfit from a photographer's studio. They wanted to surprise the boy's grandmother with a portrait in "national costume" as a keepsake. Alessandro ripped the clothes off. He was generally cooperative, but it was he who chose what games who would play.

Nonna Jacqueline was happy even without the portrait. "I don't need a photograph," she said gaily. "He is here in the flesh. Maybe one day you could come and live here. There's no Fascism here; not in our country."

The idea of moving to that place with all those canals and windmills that you only ever saw on postcards, filled her with dread. And then there was this fixation with Fascists! It wasn't that bad in Italy; you just had to steer clear of them. In any case, she would never be able to live with her mother-in-law. The woman was bizarre. Her arms were skinny and her shoulders narrow, but she leapt around like the dry twigs in the stove. Emilia was honest enough to confess to herself that seeing that old woman, who spent her days curved over a workbench and in the evening talked about what she had achieved that day as if she were reciting a poem, made her feel dull, like some sort of boring housewife with nothing to say. Perhaps it was also because of the French, which she hardly understood, never mind spoke!

Mother and son were in the same business. They cut and polished diamonds to make rings. That was why they got along so well. Marc said his mother was the true artist, but back in Genoa who had ever heard of Mrs. Jacqueline Rimon?

At least Marc's success had been noted in the city. He was free to do his work he was passionate, well organized, and fair. He also earned enough to be able to set aside a nest egg for their old age. His sense of humor was low-key, and usually aimed only at the person he was speaking to, which people appeared to appreciate. Clients brought in their most precious gemstones and refused point-blank to accept a receipt. They trusted him. Emilia knew all this, and her brother-in-law never failed to remind her, but you can't love a man just because his clients love him.

After the first few months of their marriage, Emilia tried picking fights with her husband to see if she could rouse him. She used to do the same at home when she was a little girl; if things were too quiet, she felt as though she was suffocating. Marc, the Dutchman, shied away from conflict, however, and never rose to the bait.

It is said that only a wise person can recognize wisdom in another, and Emilia was certainly not in the best position to recognize it in her husband. She had first placed him in the category of the weak. She tried giving him orders, claiming her rights, but his only reaction was an intimation of amused forbearance that drove her crazy. Every victory was transformed into defeat. The only result was to obtain what she had never wanted. She couldn't even argue with Cesarina, the housekeeper. She would rebuke her harshly sometimes, too harshly she knew, but the girl had been used to receiving blows to the back of her neck from her mother in the village where she came from. In comparison, the Rimon household was like Paradise.

Her hostility was thus left to wander freely around the house, invading the corridors like a bad smell. Other rooms were contaminated, too. They had lived like this for days and then years, convinced that the undeclared war between them would mark their destiny. One day though, everything changed suddenly. One bang and a great light had filled their horizon, like fireworks at *goyim* saint's days.

It was the boy. Their boy. He had only turned a few pages of the book of his life and there he was, just turned four, already able to read and write, invent, and recite with the same versatility as the curly-haired son in some Polish *shtetl*. It was not Hebrew in his case, but that didn't matter. The two of them, as his parents, had suddenly become close, racing almost hand-in-hand to keep up with their child prodigy.

CHAPTER 4

Alessandro only found out much later that he had had a brother. There had been another son, though he had died as a baby. Emilia had never spoken to him about it. It's not the kind of thing you talk to a child about.

His mother had been very affectionate. She couldn't stop gazing at him, and when he'd been ill, she had slept on a cot by his bedside. He didn't need a brother or a sister. He had a gang of friends on this street: Giamba, the doorman's son, and Nino, Vittorio, and Salvatore, the youngest son of the coalman who delivered blocks of ice wrapped in tea towels in the summer. They would draw a track on the road with chalk and recreate the Giro d'Italia by flicking bottle tops filled with candle wax along it. As soon as he got back home, though, silence filled the air. There was never much chatter in the house; it wasn't their habit.

His cousins, who lived two doors down on the same street, would often accompany him when he went out. Actually, only one of his cousins lived there; she was his only real cousin. Her name was Adriana. The other girl, Renata, was related to Adriana on her father's side, and she always said she was no relation at all to Alessandro. Alessandro never got it. The one who was "no relation at all" was the one he liked best, and so he'd considered her his favorite cousin.

They had always played together, the three of them. Then the girls, who were two years older than him, had had to go to school. Nowadays, they would sit at the table together doing their homework. They totally ignored him.

*

He had dragged a chair without making any noise and placed it next to Renata. The two girls didn't turn around, but they were just pretending. They were flattered that a boy would want to sit there, admiring them while they were doing their writing. Alessandro had started to imitate their every movement. He traced out lines of straight sticks on a sheet of paper and then copied out pages and pages of consonants and vowels, putting them together to make "little words". When they read out loud, his voice was right behind theirs as if he'd been invited to join in the chanting at the synagogue. The cousins thought it was an echo, his voice shadowing the words they had just uttered. Once, though, they exchanged glances and, on a signal, suddenly stopped reading. The words continued fluently, one voice sounding more resonant than three. A gasp of incredulous surprise filled the room as the girls started laughing and prancing around.

"You can read too! You can read too!" Renata chanted. "What's this letter? And this word? What about this line?" Adriana leafed quickly through the schoolbook, showing him one page after another, in the same manner as when she bossed her fluffy white puppy Mizzi around: "Stand! Hold up your paw!" Alessandro was elated by their elation and rolled about in it as happily as when he threw himself onto the wet sand at the beach. It wasn't success that excited him; it was the idea that he had managed to make them laugh. Then he started making up stories, strange puns and songs that made no sense but rhymed well. The girls couldn't stop laughing.

It was the next generation up, the girls' mothers, that delivered the news to the Rimon household. Emilia ran to the store to buy a children's book with colorful pictures. Alessandro read all the words first, and only then looked at the pictures. Emilia thought, "Somebody wants to compensate me," and then she thought, "It must be true, then, that the fabric of my life had gaping holes before." This "somebody", given that she went to services every Saturday, could well be God. She thanked him, and, while she was at it, she made peace with everyone else in the house.

Marc was next to hear about the prodigy. His eyes shone with a shadow of melancholy, as if he were contemplating something from a great distance. He went out too, and came back with a bigger book, with a black and gray cover and no pictures, entitled *Vingt mille lieues sous les mers*.

"What are you doing?" his wife shouted. "The kid has just started reading, and you're giving him a book for adults, written in French?" She sounded annoyed, but she didn't look it. She was unable to conceal a flash of pride in the challenge.

Alessandro read the book. He read it slowly, but he got to the end. He understood every word, every line. Of course, Emilia muttered, feigning an indignation which was, by now, well rehearsed. The boy's father had always had the bad habit of speaking to him in French. Maybe it was his way of reminding him of his relation to that mother who was in Holland but, to make things complicated, had been born in Belgium, and certainly thought more about her work than about her son.

All that was needed now was for the "phenomenon" to be set into a reality beyond the family circle. That was where Benito Mussolini came into it.

History had taken a small side step.

In another kind of apartment, in Rome rather than Genoa, the youngest son of the head of government and leader of the National Fascist Party, Romano Mussolini, was behaving very much like Alessandro Rimon. In 1932, just as he was turning five, he could already read and write perfectly, and the Ministry of Education was only too happy to authorize his skipping a year and starting First Grade. It's hard to make a law for just one person a law so, if there was anyone else the same age blessed with the same talent, they were allowed to do the same.

Alessandro thus found himself in First Grade, a full year younger than the rest of the class. When the teacher sent for his parents, Emilia got a fright. "Is there something wrong?" she asked. The teacher said "yes," which worried even Marc. In First Grade they learn to draw rows of straight lines and then they learn the letters and vowel sounds . . . Well, Emilia thought, losing her patience, they knew that.

"The child can already do everything. He's bored," the teacher said, shaking her head, as if she were somehow offended by the situation. She had big, round eyes in a face that was too thin; two features that were not made to go together. She's not stable, Emilia thought, her hackles rising.

"I'm putting him up a grade!" the teacher almost shouted at them. She wasn't sure herself whether it was a punishment or a compliment.

Thus, one morning when he was only just five, Alessandro Rimon, text books and exercise books in one hand and an empty satchel in the other, vacated his First-Grade desk and sat down in the Second-Grade classroom. The parents had to buy him new exercise books with lines rather than squares. He also asked for new pencils, pens, and colors, otherwise what was in it for him?

On the first day, the kids deigned him with no more than a lazy, sleepy glance. They soon realized, though, that he knew how to make them laugh.

At home now, swirls of wind blew in unexpected gusts. They were not used to it. Words, rhymes, and disconnected phrases whirled around in the air. The old man had started to join in, spurring his grandson on.

Words were no longer enough. Tangible, everyday objects were dragged into their joyful tirades. Rice, for example.

Alessandro would only eat it when the moon was big and round. It wasn't a spoilt child's whimsy; he knew what he wanted and asked for it, almost begging. Embarrassed and proud, the family gave in to his requests. It wasn't such a bad thing to have a little corner of madness in the house, after all. It got to the point where everyone raced to put the rice on the stove at full moon.

Who knows how many kids there were scattered around the country following Romano Mussolini and Alessandro Rimon's example? As with love, each family was convinced their own child was unique. How can anyone believe that the love that moves them could be the same in others?

Alessandro *was* a little genius, but he didn't turn into a genius. He was just a kid who had started to run too soon and one day had suddenly grown tired. The fire was reduced to a flame that still crackled but at a normal, acceptable intensity.

CHAPTER 5

Aunt Wanda and her husband, Osvaldo, had no children. A "phenomenon" of a nephew was compensation. "Look what happened to us: a kid like that," they would murmur when they met people, feigning detachment, almost apologizing, as if their nephew had pulled a fast one on them.

Osvaldo was a good-looking man, with curly hair that looked as though it was going gray as a joke, and the deportment of a master of ceremonies at the royal court. A true Genoese gentleman, people would say, even though he wasn't from Genoa. He had been born and bred in Livorno, but Genoa had given him a *place*. The Nunes family business was the most successful jeweler's in the city. The client base included all the men of property and spirit of the day, in addition to their wives and lovers; predictably, most of them nurtured good relations with the regime. It wasn't polite to refer to this, of course. None of them were actually Fascist hierarchs; it was sufficient to be *acquainted* with one.

Alessandro was given an essay to write in class: "Why I love the *Duce*." The boy threw himself into the task wholeheartedly. The result was a portrait of a man who was half his father and half his Uncle Osvaldo—he had even thrown in the curly graying hair—but he wrote it with such passion that the teacher gave him top marks. She didn't notice that the tall, silent, wise man bore no similarity to Benito Mussolini whatsoever.

She simply appreciated the talent of her little pupil, who was so much younger than the others. It was not a coincidence, in fact, that he was selected to recite the Fascist Oath in the name of the whole school at the assembly hall, dressed in the full *Balilla* uniform. He was then taken to Rome with the rest of the class to applaud the *Duce* in real life under his balcony in Piazza Venezia. The teacher was unable to go as she had to take care of her own young children, who both had sore throats and had gotten ill just as she was due to leave. Her class lined up in full uniform, representing the bravado of the Fascist spring. They were her pride and joy.

On his return to Genoa, Alessandro started attending the Saturday rallies at Piazza della Vittoria again. He didn't know what was happening to him, though. Everything around him was the same, but something inside him had changed. The parts of his body no longer seemed to communicate. It felt as though his feet and hands had gone to sleep and had stopped obeying any commands. His uniform was soaked in sweat, even when there was no sun. His thoughts were trammeled and unable to get out even in confused fragments. Finally, he understood. The monster paralyzing him was boredom. Waiting hours and hours in a square where someone was supposed to arrive, without even knowing who. Maybe they didn't exist. They might never arrive.

One Saturday, he took a step towards the edge of the piazza, then another, faster one. Once he was around the corner, he started running.

He never went to the rally again, and nobody noticed. He didn't like the leader of the *Balilla* youth movement in any case: he was always trying to touch up the boys.

Their son was no longer going to the Saturday rallies. Emilia was worried; Marc gave her a half-smile.

"Have you ever talked to him about politics?" For a long time now, she adopted a tone of inquiry rather than an accusation.

"No, no." Marc was defensive anyway. "I wouldn't want him to get into trouble at school."

And yet, who was it who read whole articles out loud to the kid from *Le Journal*, that French newspaper with such a banal name? That rag didn't exactly pay compliments to the Fascist regime. He'd also been telling Alessandro the story of the Spanish Revolution, as if it were a weekly comic strip, with the brigades fighting on the side of the "goodies" and general Franco with the Fascists being cast as the "baddies"! Italians, incidentally, were Franco's allies. They could only pray that the topic of the Spanish war wouldn't come up at school. Did Marc know anything about his son, or had he no idea what he was like? They all knew that since he was a baby, Alessandro had always latched onto certain words. Now that he was into the Spanish war, he was fixated with a French term for the "good" fighters: *gouvernementaux*. He said the word over and over again, maybe because it had so many syllables, and it made him feel as if he were playing scales up and down on the piano. Only someone as clueless as her husband could believe that no, he wasn't instilling political ideas in his son's mind. Not at all.

Luckily, one day, Marc had another idea. He brought home a comic—finally something for children. It was called *L'avventuroso*. That's how you make a child happy. Finally, Alessandro was talking about Gordon and his eternal fiancée, Dale, and about Cino and Franco. Adventures, in short. Nothing else.

Staying out of politics in those days was wise, but not always easy to achieve. There was always someone in the family ready to go off on a rant. Carlo, for example, a "cousin" of some degree or other—they were all cousins anyway—had been stubbornly enrolled in the Communist Party since he first opened his eyes on the world. It may have been because they dealt with coal and fire all their lives, but all the Genoese railway workers were that way inclined. It was Carlo's fault if, whenever there was a rally in the city for some hotshot in the country, he ended up spending a couple of nights in a prison cell. He hadn't lost his job with the railway, and he should have been grateful for that, even though he had been demoted to working in a warehouse, stacking used spare parts.

Luigi had also been a railway man but, luckily, he'd retired too early to become a Communist.

One evening, Osvaldo and his wife arrived at the house a great deal earlier than usual. It wasn't his style to be out of breath, but this time Osvaldo looked as if he'd run up the four flights of stairs in a hurry. "Our cousin Bruna just called. She's desperate. Her son has disappeared." After a pause, he added, muttering with his head bowed, "She says the Fascists must have arrested him."

CHAPTER 6

W ho do you mean?" Emilia butted in immediately. "The Fausto we know? The one who claims he's studying at university at the same time as working in his parents' store?" She shook her head. "Anti-Fascist, him? What stories are you believing now?"

"All you need to do is make a joke about it. That would be just like him," Marc murmured. "If anyone makes anti-Fascist comments, they are interned, and certainly not quietly," he explained—more to himself than to the others.

"Of course. These punishments are supposed to serve as an example," Osvaldo said, more patiently than he felt.

It was so annoying . . . Emilia was churning. Men always ended up talking about politics! Fausto must have gone off for his own reasons. What did it have it to do with Osvaldo anyway? The lad wasn't exactly in the inner circle of cousins.

"Osvaldo knows a lot of people," Wanda sighed, answering the question her sister hadn't even uttered.

"My sister's always putting her husband on a pedestal," Emilia brooded, unhappy to have had her thoughts exposed. "I suppose the down-town jeweler's gives her some perks, like special invitations and tickets to boring old shows. But is that really enough to admire a man who chooses going to the *osteria* with his father and brother-in-law over you? A man who comes over every evening to pick these people up?"

Emilia stopped. It was as if the thought was trying to coax her into a smile. In the house there was a child, a little genius, who had become the star attraction for the whole family. That's why everyone wanted to come over.

Old Luigi was just outside the door, in silence. Looking. Listening. "Just look at you all," he reflected. "You're holding a family meeting, whatever it's about, and who shows up first? Your stupid weaknesses. Uninvited guests, like greyhounds breaking out of their traps at the starting gun. That's who. Keep your girlish expectations, petty jealousies, lack of affection, and unsubstantiated dreams under control, for once! That's enough, now. You're adults. Luckily, at the age of eighty, I can watch these games from the outside."

Seemingly, none of them had spared a thought for a family that had, one way or another, lost a son.

This was not the case, however. Osvaldo had taken action. He'd checked the main police station and hospitals, just as the family had done, but he had redoubled their efforts by using a few contacts, which were decidedly more influential. The result was the same, however. Fausto Passigli did not appear on any registry of deaths, accidents, or arrests anywhere in the country.

Had he gone into hiding? This hypothesis needed examining, Osvaldo said.

Luigi made it clear that it was his turn to intervene. Since he had been a railway man, too, it made him feel one with his cousin Carlo and thus an integral part of the Communist Party.

One evening he came home very late and sat in his usual rush-bottomed chair at the kitchen table. His cousin Carlo had been happy to see him. He had hugged him several times and told him about a new wine dealer who delivered to the house. The wine was good: he had tried it.

He didn't mention anything else and nobody asked.

The sisters had gone to see Bruna and Alberto Passigli, Fausto's parents. They talked of nothing else on the way, agreeing completely. The family insisted on finding obscure political motivations, pinning everything on current events, when in Emilia's and Wanda's view the explanation for his disappearance was personal: Fausto Passigli had run off for reasons that were his alone.

When they got to the house, however, their attitude quickly changed. Idle chatter had to be pushed away and squashed into the background. The mother's face was like a mask: tears gushed never-endingly over a painted heart-shaped mouth—a lifetime's habit, no doubt. The father was sitting completely still, sobbing.

Emilia and Wanda went back home, their heads bowed, their steps heavy. Mystery deserved the utmost respect because at the end of the path one might come upon a little hole dug out by a child, or a bottomless chasm pulling one into its depths.

Months went by, the days both too long and too quick. Once the gritty determination of the early days was over, the search had run aground. Everyone except Fausto's parents felt the urgency less keenly, as though it had faded.

But one day it happened. Alessandro recognized his cousin across the street in a distant part of the city, where his mother had dragged him to chase up her old seamstress who had moved houses. "Mamma, look!" he shouted excitedly, yanking at his mother's arm. "There's our cousin who's been kidnapped!"

Emilia turned around and saw Fausto Passigli, turned to stone, right there in front of her.

He was standing there, his hair as uncombed as when he was a boy, in a coat and tie and an unusual pair of big, brown shoes, gasping as if someone had stolen the portion of air that was his by right. There were no signs that he had been wounded or come to harm in any way.

He didn't greet her. Instead, he leaned over to whisper something to the glamorous brunette standing next to him. In her turn, she squared them up, scanning mother and child in a way that was both vague and piercing.

CHAPTER 7

It was clear that Fausto had not yet decided how to react. Nobody had ever seen him being aggressive. Confused, yes; quite often.

"Emilia," he said weakly, more of a statement than an address. He said he no longer lived in Genoa and traveled for work between the Liguria region and Milan. At that time, he was living in Milan. He had thrown the titbit into the conversation as if to say, "Here are the pieces, put them together if you wish." He was a salesman for a company that produced hardware and mechanical components, he explained in a reassured tone, almost brazen.

He turned and indicated with the palm of his hand the brunette standing next to him, who was as calm and indifferent as she had been before. "I've learned everything from her, she's very good," he said in a sweeter tone. "Her name is Jole." It was evident that uttering her name gave him a thrill of pleasure.

Emilia did not consider this an introduction and didn't put her hand out.

Off the bat, the boy said, "I'm Alessandro. Do you remember me? Did you go and join the Spanish Revolution?"

"Me? No, I found a job where I could earn a lot of money. You know? I'll only go back home when I'm rich." Fausto directed his words to the boy but was smirking at Emilia.

She could take it no longer. "You!" she yelled. "Did you really have to run away to peddle scrap metal? Did you need to vanish into thin air, throwing your family into despair?"

Fausto continued to address the boy, but his chin wobbled slightly as he spoke. He told him a story about a swallow who had made its nest in the gutters of a building, and who felt free and self-sufficient there; if the building hadn't been there, the bird would never have been able to make its nest. "You see," he added hastily, "That's how I feel. They wanted to make me feel independent, but everything I've ever had has come from my parents . . . the apartment, my studio, my job . . . You must be able to see why I left, right?"

Alessandro stared at him. He didn't understand what the man was trying to achieve. If it was a story, I wasn't a very good one. He much preferred the foreign ones his father read to him.

Fausto darkened visibly as he realized that the boy—more importantly the woman towards whom his justification had really been aimed—had not appreciated his efforts. "I get that you're a relative," he said, veering menacingly towards Emilia. "But who cares? Really, just because I bump into you by chance on a damned sidewalk, doesn't mean I have to give you chapter and verse about my life, does it?"

The young woman had been standing there watching them. She hadn't looked shocked, or even interested. Now and again she'd tucked a few locks back into her hairdo after the unexpected breeze straight from the sea had blown them out of place. Fausto grabbed her by the elbow and started to pull her away. They had already gotten to the end of the sidewalk by the time Emilia's response reached them. "You do have to tell me about your life, because I'm the one who's been consoling your mother for days and months."

They were soon hurrying back home. "No seamstress?" the boy asked. Emilia picked up her pace.

She asked her husband to call Osvaldo and tell him to come over immediately. It was urgent.

Marc stared at her. Did they really have to wait for their brother-in-law before they could talk? The answer was before his eyes, so why bother wasting time only to be humiliated?

"Jole what? What's her family name?" It was as if this was the only thing in the whole incredible story that piqued Osvaldo's interest. A missing piece. Without a last name, there was no way of finding out who the woman was. She had to be the source of everything . . . He looked miserably—one could say murderously—at his sister-in-law and even at the child. Emilia quivered with indignation. She wasn't used to this treatment. It was usually her giving other people a dressing down.

He asked Alessandro straight out what the woman looked like. Did she look like your mother? Your aunt? Your teacher?

Alessandro shouted an outraged "No!", and his uncle understood.

"We didn't have the chance to ask her what her last name was," Emilia defended herself crossly. "Let them work it out themselves," she muttered. "Let them work it out if they're as clever as they think they are."

Happy days and dark days followed. Among the closest family members, joy and desperation had twisted and tangled itself into a tight knot. Find him, find him; no, we don't want to hear another word about him. He ran away like Cain; may God forgive him. He's a fragile soul. He's *alive*. The fact remained that he would never be allowed to darken their door again. Bruna and Alberto Passigli would carry on their lives as though they no longer had a son.

The rest of the family had towed the line with solicitous attention.

Jole Mantelli was officially an ironware saleswoman, but her connections to the Genoa and Milan-based crime syndicates had been noted. The fact that she was currently cohabiting with a young man from a bourgeois family had also been registered. There was no available information regarding the young man's links with her underworld collaborators.

Osvaldo had managed to gather the salient information and reconstruct the couple's history. Years earlier, a mechanism that facilitated the opening and closing of curtains had come onto the market. It appeared that the attractive young Jole had been the one to demonstrate its effectiveness in the curtain store that Fausto's parents ran. Fausto had been working that day.

"There's someone for you in the hall." Emilia made sure her face was expressionless, but nobody even noticed as it had become her normal countenance. Who? She had no inkling or, at least, that's what it looked like.

Fausto.

Marc couldn't believe his eyes. Then he murmured, "You can't come here. The family all agrees: they don't want to see you."

"I know. I came to see you precisely because you're foreign."

There was something honest about this answer, and Marc was confused because the young man was trying—with some difficulty—to explain that the French were more open-minded, possibly owing to the Enlightenment or the Revolution. "I'm not French," Marc wanted to say, but what was the point of answering back when the clarification probably didn't interest young Fausto in the slightest?

Fausto suddenly started talking. He wasn't standing on any old sidewalk now; he had come specially to tell him all about his life. Marc prodded him in the back, guiding him to his study. When he pointed at a chair, Fausto dropped himself onto it as if he had always longed for that very gesture and sought out that haven.

He told him about the small apartment his parents had

bought for him so that he could study in peace, the law degree that he was struggling to obtain, his part-time job in the family store. His parents had seemingly encouraged him to deal with suppliers, but everybody knew it was all a sham. When he was a child, they used to make him recite a poem whenever the family got together. One day he had had the good fortune to meet Jole; it had been one of those encounters that come along once in a lifetime. Everything else had stemmed from that first meeting. He worked with her and was making a lot of money. He had already saved quite a bit, and this had contributed to making him almost happy.

Marc listened and was taken over by a vague sense of animosity, mixed with suppressed affection. "Did you really need to run away to achieve all of this?" It was the same question his wife had yelled out on a street in the suburbs of the city.

"When you dive into the sea, you do it in one fell swoop; you don't cut through the air in stages." Fausto looked pleased with the metaphor, and Marc smiled, remembering the story his son had told him about the swallows in the gutter. "I'd planned to go back to my family once I'd gained a secure footing, but things didn't work out that way," young Fausto mumbled, less sure of himself now. He showed no inclination whatsoever to leave. There was still Jole to talk about. He knew that there'd been gossip about the company he was keeping. Things were simpler than they seemed. Jole's father had grown up in a working-class neighborhood of Milan. He had been an honest ironmonger and locksmith, but not all his friends had been as honest as he was. Some had ended up in jail. Friends are friends, however, and after he died, the gang had poured all their attentions on Jole. She had been left alone as a young girl since her mother had gone to live in Nice years before. They only spoke occasionally. The girl had had to fend for herself, and if there remained a little affection from her father's friends, what was the harm in that?

It was getting late. The clattering of saucepans and plates could be heard from the back of the house. Marc got up slowly. Fausto looked concerned: he had so many things still to ask. He had intended to ask Marc a few details about the tools on his workbench. He had been staring at them throughout his long ramble.

Fausto stood up, too, holding out his arm in an abrupt gesture. It wasn't a salute; in his fingers he held a card with something scribbled on it by hand. "My address in Milan," he said drily. "Below that, there's the telephone number for my Genoa apartment. It belongs to a relative but she's never there. We're the only ones . . ."

Marc was uncertain. Taking his card felt like a gesture of reconciliation on the part of the family. He didn't think he was authorized to act on their behalf.

"You might need it . . ." Fausto said, in a firm decisive voice for the first time. He added vaguely, ". . . for some supplies, perhaps." But the look on his face, Marc thought as he said those last words, looked sarcastic, conspiratorial, even.

It was almost dark now; no, it couldn't be that.

CHAPTER 8

"There's a paper I need you to go out and buy for me," his father said one Sunday morning.

"Is it a newspaper you're not allowed to buy?" Alessandro asked excitedly.

"It's not one of the banned ones. I wouldn't ask you, of all people, if it were," Marc explained hastily. "It's the Vatican daily."

"I certainly wouldn't get a kid involved," Emilia hissed. "Since you've done so without even asking me, at least give him a reason. Our son is quite intelligent."

Marc needed no further encouragement. He had a mountain of ideas that he wanted to test out, and being able to do so with his son was his greatest desire. He wasn't pushing him. No longer going to the Fascist rallies had been the kid's own choice.

He settled into his chair and abandoned himself to his explanation. *L'Osservatore Romano* was the official organ of the Vatican, a foreign state that was therefore free to publish news from Italy that other newspapers were not allowed to print. French papers were no longer available, so reading *L'Osservatore Romano* was important to find out what was really happening in the world. Simple, right? The newsagent, however, may grow suspicious if he saw the same person regularly buying one paper rather than another. A kid doesn't know anything, so who would ask him?

Alessandro was very pleased to be involved in the plot. He perfected the plan by buying *L'Osservatore Romano* together with his comic, *L'avventuroso,* and a humorous rag called *Bertoldo.* He stuck his father's daily between the other two weeklies. Walking as fast as he could down the street, he felt like a jailbird's accomplice, smuggling a file into prison in a cheese sandwich.

Marc began to feel it was his duty to read his son the "real" news that he managed to glean here and there from the papers, just as he found the finest stones to cut. He would never give up *Acta Diurna.* The author had a rare ability to cloak his subtle attacks on Fascism with clichés and naive comments. [1] Alessandro was as enthralled by the noble art of saying something without actually saying it as he used to be with the word *gouvernementaux.* He had learned to read by observing his cousins. It had been like learning musical notes. He now felt ready to start using the notes to compose music and perform it.

Every day their teacher, Maestra Giacinta, would give them an essay to write in class. They were preparing for their elementary-school final exams. One morning she wrote a phrase on the board: "Italy, Italy sacred in the new dawn, between the plough and the ship's bow." The children rubbed their eyes. A few scoffed, one boy acted as if his hand was paralyzed, another started to whimper. The keen blonde girls were the only ones hunched zealously over their notebooks scribbling furiously, blowing their hair out of their eyes at intervals.

Alessandro glanced at his desk-mate's test sheet. He had started with, "The Fascist nation is giving an important lesson to the world," and then he had not known what else to write. For Alessandro, however, like for the Ivory Patrol in his adventure comic, the time had come. He was going to write his own

---

[1] The author, Guido Gonella, became a minister of the Italian Republic after the war.

Acta Diurna. He would be diplomatic and subtle, a true master of masked discourse.

The teacher called him aside the following day. "Your essay was very good. Not one mistake," she said, although her expression did not match her words. She handed him a blank sheet with nothing but 10/10 written on it. "Write what you're supposed to write," she said, already turning away.

Alessandro was not offended; disappointed, perhaps. He had put his plan into action. He had tried. Maybe the "saying" had outweighed the "not saying" in this attempt. He had no problem writing another composition. All he had to do was open his arms and catch the readily formed words that were floating around in his head. He wasn't upset with Maestra Giacinta. She was kind, in a placid sort of way, like plentiful quantities of bread and milky coffee in the morning.

There were many girl cousins and aunts in the family. Alessandro really only cared about Adriana and the other girl, Renata, who wasn't even a cousin. Adriana and Renata had leaped with joy and chanted when they'd realized they'd taught their baby cousin to read without even knowing it. Now the girls were in Middle School; one of them even had a secret, poorly matched boyfriend. The halo of little genius had hovered above Alessandro's head over the years. He had not needed his cousins' help for a long time; these days they would only ever bump into one another by chance.

When the news started to spread that Alessandro had been the one to find their missing relative, the girls had come to see him. But it wasn't him; he'd done nothing at all. He'd just spotted him on the other side of the road. The girls grilled him, asking urgent questions about the brunette who had been out and about with their cousin Fausto. Did he really not remember any other details, not even the color of her dress? He remembered her high heels. That he did. She was beautiful, wasn't she? Renata had whispered, almost embarrassed. Alessandro had said yes, with the same flush in his cheeks.

They came back to claim what was theirs by right when the time came for his end-of-school exam. It was a trifling test for him. The admissions test for Middle School worried him far more. It meant going to a big school where he would have more than one teacher; none of whom he knew, all of whom were strict. Since the cousins had been the ones to discover he was a genius, they felt it was their duty to go on polishing all the different facets of the creature they had trained.

Drawing was not his strong point. The scribbles of the children at nursery school were the fruits of the most wonderful imaginations, while Alessandro's were an insult to both pencil and paper. Renata made him draw the same landscape for days: a little house, a hill, a pine tree. The drawing he produced in his test was childlike but almost up to standard. The teacher he handed it in to smiled through his teeth.

His grades for the end of Elementary School exam were off the charts; his admissions exam for Middle School was average.

CHAPTER 9

His mother took him on the first day. Alessandro had been accepted at a branch of the main school, in one of the narrow passageways in the old town. He loved wandering through the crisscrossing alleys, where oblique rays of sunshine alternated with shadows. Emilia didn't like it one bit. It would have been much more convenient and logical if the boy had been assigned to the main school. It was a big place, with a stellar reputation, and all his classmates had been admitted there. He would have been much better off, for sure.

The janitor stopped them as they approached. "The Elementary School is at the end of the road on the right," he said grudgingly.

"We're headed for the Middle School," his mother bridled. The janitor threw up his arms as if to say, "Be my guest."

In class, a girl and two boys were chatting among themselves in a group. They turned around and glanced at the kid who had just walked in and then turned back to what they had been doing. They clearly knew one another already.

The girl, who would probably turn into a beauty one day, with light chestnut-colored hair that curled inwards at shoulder level, had left the group to go and talk to another girl. She turned and walked towards Alessandro lazily, staring at him as he cowed at the door.

"Are you sure you didn't come to the wrong school?" she asked in a superior but kind tone.

"No. I did the exam and I was admitted to Middle School,"

Alessandro answered hastily and nervously. When she asked, "How old are you?" He bowed his head and said "Nine."

"Listen up!" the girl yelled to the others. "There's a kid in our class the same age as my baby brother."

They all stared, openly hostile. They were fed up with younger siblings. As it was, they were struggling to kick themselves free of the younger child that inhabited them still. Finding an exemplar in flesh and bone in their class threw them; it made them feel they were moving backwards rather than forwards.

Alessandro went and sat next to a boy sitting on his own in silence. The boy had no intention of speaking to an intruder like him, protecting his self-imposed silence in case the new boy wanted to sabotage it. His desk-mate was stooped over a math book. Being permanently sunk into his calculations must have been the most he ever asked of life.

When school was over, Emilia was waiting for him at the gate. Alessandro answered in monosyllables on their way home. His mother got the message and, after a while, stopped trying to talk to him. She was upset. She'd waited so long for this day to come.

The following morning, four bullies who sat at the back of the class were waiting in the corridor as Alessandro came in.

"Where's your Mommy? Does she wait for you like a good mommy all day in the hall?" They rocked back and forth sucking their thumbs like babies in daycare. One of them even had a pacifier in his mouth. He pulled the thing out, dripping with saliva, and tried to stick it between Alessandro's lips.

He asked his mother never to take him to school again. She said she had no intention of letting him go alone. "You're not ten yet," she reminded him. "We'll see next year."

Another practical joke became popular in class, invented by an ugly kid who was small but the right age for the class. Every time he saw Alessandro, he would give him a thump on the shoulder and, instead of saying "ciao," he would bawl like a newborn: "waah-waah." The whole class had started to greet him by wailing "waah-waah."

Some of the class, especially the girls, thought they were being benevolent, affectionate even. Alessandro pretended to laugh with them. Some of the teachers remembered that the kid had passed his exams early, but none of them were particularly curious. The Liberal Arts teacher, Mrs. Vivaldi, looked on with some satisfaction, and just a hint of pique, whenever the diminutive pupil raised his hand like a flash to answer some question about Italian literature or history. He never once let another classmate get there first. It wasn't to show off. She knew it must be a game of sorts.

It had been a game throughout Elementary School. The kids had loved it. They used to laugh whenever he managed to pull a word out of thin air. The whole class had urged him on. They'd applauded him as they would one of those contestants on the radio who always won the quizzes. Alessandro had felt as popular and loved as those contestants. He'd thought things would go on the same way in big school.

He looked at his new classmates. They sighed and rolled their eyes every time he answered a question quicker than lightning, shouting in a voice that was maybe too squeaky. They were no longer satisfied with their usual jokes. They started teasing him because he didn't take part in religious education lessons. "Lucky you," they would taunt, whenever he came in an hour later, or was allowed out an hour early, according to the timetable. Then they would weigh in with the killer question, "Were you born in Jerusalem?"

"I'm as Genoese as you are," he could have said but never did. He didn't want to take part in their stupid teasing.

The girl with the hair that curled inwards was called

Daniela. Every now and again, she would go back to being friendly, as she had been on the first day. One day she asked him, "Would you be able to write two different essays on the same subject quickly?" Alessandro suddenly felt that brighter times might be ahead. She needed help on a class test. He wrote two compositions in the allotted time and handed one over to her. "Can I put my name on it?" she whispered.

They both got 9/10. Daniela was thrilled by the coincidence. They became friends. One day, he heard her confabulating with her friends about a birthday party. Alessandro had not been invited. He supposed the occasion was just for girls.

During lessons he was numb; sometimes he felt like he was sleep-walking. Italian and History were his favorite subjects, and he was still able to engage, but the other lessons were like listening to something happening on the other side of a thick wall. There were times when he didn't even bother to listen. He would stare out of the narrow windows, even though there was nothing to look at but the gray wall of the building opposite, and a couple of pigeons attempting to perch on a window sill or a jutting brick.

He was trying to keep peddling on his brightly colored bike, but it was falling apart as he rode it through the streets, and he knew it would soon stop working altogether.

Mrs. Vivaldi called Alessandro's parents to come and see her. Emilia arrived in the shade of her best hat, the one with the ruched rose-red ribbon. She was preening, expecting to be regaled in the new school with the same praise she had always welcomed with open arms in the old one. Her expression, as usual, betrayed a mixture of modesty and pride.

That morning, however, the teacher set off on an altogether different tack: she wanted to impress on Emilia how important Latin was in Roman—nay, in universal—culture. Didn't the teacher know that she wasn't interested in generic divagations of that kind? What was the woman saying? This new teacher wasn't even worth Maestra Giacinta's pinkie. Difficulty with Latin, eh? Now she was harping on about other subjects that weren't even hers to talk about. Math, Science; she thinks she can even discuss Technical Drawing. Well, let her talk; Emilia wasn't going to listen. Her thoughts were waylaid by a niggling conviction that she should get her eyes tested soon. There were swarms of dark spots chasing one another in front of her eyes, and her legs were hurting, too.

"I haven't said anything that bad," the teacher said, noticing the stunned look on the mother's face. "You're taking things too seriously. Your son won't fail the year; it's just that his results are not as brilliant as you were used to in Elementary School." After a pause, in a softer voice, she asked, "Why did you decide to send him to Middle School so early?"

The only thing Emilia managed to say to regain her dignity was, "It wasn't us. The school decided for us. He was too clever to wait another year." Finally, she would be able to get up and leave.

Mrs. Vivaldi stopped her. "Can I give you some advice?" she asked. "There must be someone at home that can help your son. Get him to do a few extra exercises in Latin."

"My husband speaks French and German but not Latin," Emilia said, liquidating the teacher's suggestion.

"Mine doesn't either," the teacher said, smiling.

Emilia had once read in a novel that when you are happy, you hear festive bells ringing in your ears. At that moment, it sounded like her ears were being hammered.

CHAPTER 10

M arc was upset, but not overly so. His son had some very high marks, which made up for the ones where he only got 60%. His grade point average would still be decent.

Wanda and Osvaldo were of the same opinion. What was the tragedy? There are highs and lows—even at work. Heavens above! Nobody should triumph all the time.

"You shouldn't have sent him to school so young," Nonno Luigi said, summing up the situation, and allowing Emilia to give him the full force of the resentment that had been boiling up inside her.

Didn't they understand? Her son wasn't some little homunculus looking for glory. Her son was a genius. Or at least he had been, once. She, Emilia Rimon, née Dello Strologo, had been convinced that it was God who had rewarded her with a gift to compensate for all the other things that hadn't gone well in her life. Had God set her up? Well, the joke's on Him. She wasn't like that Job guy, who accepted all the misfortunes that God rained down on him to test his devotion. Before all this, she half-believed in God. Now she didn't. It was fine. She would carry on going to the synagogue on the Sabbath, though. She didn't want people to imagine there were problems in the family. Maybe no one knew that her boy had become normal in his first year of big school. The mediocre gloat when they can see themselves reflected in others who are equally mediocre.

As for the family, well! Her sister, Wanda, once in a blue moon dined on some wealthy person's terrace with a sea view and believed she'd been invited to court. Her husband, Osvaldo, was just as bad, dressing like an ambassador to the King and acting the part too. Her old father thought he was wise just because he was old. And Marc, her husband? He was too indulgent, always ready to cave in. Like with their cousin, who had been seen on the arm of a wanton woman, a *goy* of the worst kind to boot, and who had dared run to him for help. Clients appreciated him, praising his seriousness and skill, but none of them were as impressive as the ones who strode imperiously into Osvaldo's jewelry store.

Then a little genius had descended into that dull family, a boy who had skipped through all the grades, arousing affection and enthusiasm wherever he went. They had all fallen for his extraordinary talent, which shone through despite the fact that he'd been born in an ordinary apartment with a workshop at the end of the hallway. They'd been so happy! Now they were all embracing his normality. Saying that change is normal. She was the only one who wasn't prepared to accept it. Never. She felt an inarticulate sense of hatred rise up inside her, filling up every space in her body. Hatred, unlike love, flows freely, the same way that red wine, once uncorked, rushes into a glass. All she could see in the future was an ordinary little boy, who was sometimes lively and intelligent, looking out into confused darkness. The little boy was her son. She would take good care of him, dutifully, as she did her husband. But she could no longer pin her hopes and dreams onto him.

Then her hatred sank back down again. All that was left was an incoherent rancor that created a film over everything, like the cover she put over the apricots laid out on the wooden board to dry in the sun.

CHAPTER 11

T he cousins were back in his life. After all, they'd been the ones to pull the little genius out of a hat. So what if it was all over? They were perfectly happy either way. They continued to laugh at Alessandro's jokes, which had the effect of winding him up and setting him off again with his improvisations. Renata had guessed there was something going on besides problems in some of his subjects. She forced him to talk. For the first time ever, the words she received in response were half swallowed, almost incomprehensible: they don't want me in class, they laugh at me, they pretend they're little babies who need their mommies when they see me, they call me *Jew*. His cousin warned him not to laugh alongside them. "You'll turn yourself into the victim they want you to be," she advised. "Being nice to them, which is what you're doing, is a double-edged sword. You think you're being friendly, but actually you're showing weakness. Ignore them."

Alessandro went back to following the pigeon's vain attempts to perch on the narrow sill. Things calmed down, but he was still excluded from the different groups of friends. For the kids from the poorest alleys, he was an irritating know-it-all; for those from the wealthier quarters of the city, he was "too young" for their get-togethers. His silent desk-mate remained silent because that was the paradise that he had chosen for himself.

In Seventh Grade, things improved. Some of his classmates asked him to help them with their Italian or History homework, and a beautifully thin girl had even offered to do a drawing for him in exchange for an Italian class essay. The drawing test came after; the girl had received her perfectly written paper days before. The day of art class, Alessandro spent the whole hour throwing paper balls at his classmates' bony shoulders. When it was time to hand in, there was only his signature on the blank sheet. Nothing else.

It was a dull morning, and the sky was uniformly gray. After staring at the facade of the building opposite, seeking out the usual pigeon, Alessandro's gaze came to rest on the nondescript wall of the classroom. The same predictable scene every day; not even a fly to stir things up a little.

In front of him, there was the brown teacher's desk stained with black ink, Mrs. Vivaldi explaining some aspect of Latin grammar, and in the middle of the wall—as in all classrooms—a crucifix with portraits of the King and of Mussolini on either side just below. These simulacra had always been there to keep him company in his hours of boredom, but it was only at that moment, on that day, that he saw them as if for the first time. They had suddenly leaped off the wall as if they had a life of their own. He felt the wisecrack swell up inside him and tried to stop it coming out, though he knew he would never succeed.

"Look! There's Christ between two thieves!" he yelled out, as if the words had unleashed themselves from the chains that had been holding them down.

The split-second's silence that followed felt as if it cloaked the entire universe. The teacher's face blanched, as if an artist unhappy with his creation had frantically applied brushstrokes of white lead to erase the portrait he had just painted. His classmates were rolling off their chairs laughing. A janitor appeared out of nowhere, summoned by who knows whom, grabbed the boy by one arm (the other was firmly held by the teacher), and dragged him to the Principal's office. The Principal was standing up, and his parents hurried in. The *matter*. It was serious, very serious. He was only a child, two years younger than the others, he didn't know what the *matter* was. The others? Did they hear? They're so stupid they laughed. A punishment was needed, but how could it be inflicted without referring to the *matter*. One could leave the reason vague: a fight, harmful behavior, insubordination? Harmful behavior was best, it could refer to a whole range of misbehaviors, including the moral kind. Suspended for five days sounds fair. The Principal wrote out the punishment as if it were a test of his handwriting. By the time Marc got home, his breath had finally returned to normal. He had been expecting jail or internment.

Alessandro went back to school five days later, and his classmates welcomed him back with grudging admiration. They called him from across the playground, patted him on the back, and acted as though they'd been friends forever. But it wasn't his political courage that had drawn them to him; they could hardly remember the incriminating comment and, anyway, Fascism was part and parcel, to varying degrees, of all of their daily lives. The fact was that their teacher had blanched in front of them: janitor, Principal, and parents had been involved; and the ensuing ballet was a welcome distraction that had amused them more than a comedy at the cinema. That was why they were patting the boy on the back; he had returned from his exile victorious.

Alessandro might well have settled happily into that class the following year.

But History decided otherwise.

CHAPTER 12

N ormality has no idea that it is normal. It advances slowly, in well-worn habits and minuscule changes. You don't even know whether you like the things you are doing.

Emilia, long before the start of summer, had booked their usual sunbed and umbrella for three months at the Benvenuto Beach Club on Corso Italia. They booked the same dates every year; it was normal for people living in a seaside town, everyone loved the place.

Then *The Four Musketeers* had come along, and all her plans had suddenly seemed less important. The characters had met with unexpected success on the radio: children and adults alike, from one end of Italy to the other, were sucked into the maelstrom in a wild crescendo of exuberant comments. The whole country was tuning in, and people talked of little else. Alessandro's household still didn't have a radio. The family was seriously considering buying a set. Alessandro went to Aunt Wanda's every day to listen to *The Four Musketeers*. He had asked whether he could bring a friend, and his aunt had said "yes" without thinking twice. Their store was in the city center, and Osvaldo never came home before the evening.

"Wash your face," Alessandro had said to Salvatore; and his friend, who had little experience of such things, had also wet his hair.

"Did they throw a pail of water at you?" Aunt Wanda laughed. The radio was already on, airing commercials.

*

The days went by, and Wanda seemed to change. She strode around the house as if she were on stage, laughing for no reason. The scenes she liked the best were the ones when the boys' eyes were wide open with fear.

She had her nephew to herself every day, sitting on her sofa, and she felt as if she had won the final battle against her sister. This was what gave her such joy, though she would never have admitted it.

She had grown fond of the radio. She left it on all day, almost as if she wanted to prolong the echo of Alessandro's presence in the house. There were times when she happened on items of political news. They nagged at her, and she started thinking about them more and more. She even started reading the papers that her husband—usually a paragon of tidiness—left strewn around the house, even on the floor.

Reading and listening, Wanda had completed the journey from the *Musketeers* to the planet of anxiety. She had slowly begun to piece together a picture. The stories the radio and newspapers told were either false, disguised, or constructed. What she had to do was strip away the coating and get down to the core. There was bound to be some divine punishment, she thought. Optimism, light-heartedness, and frivolity—the younger sisters of joy—run away and hide when understanding creeps in.

They came one evening. They could hear their steps from the stairs they were so heavy. It was too early for the men's usual evening escape to the *osteria*; the family had not yet had dinner. Wanda was the first to come in.

She had a small light and dark-blue striped bag with a golden zipper tucked under her arm that Emilia had never seen before; it must have been new. She was anxiously clutching a bundle of newspapers folded into three in her other hand. Osvaldo was hot on her heels, looking surly and ready for a fight. His wife dropped into an armchair and spread the newspapers out on her lap like a street hawker.

"Have you seen the news?" she shrieked. "They're all talking about the Jews." Almost in a whisper, she went on, "Did you know that there are too many of us? Are things starting here, like in Germany?" She was in a terrible state. That was the only explanation for her running up the stairs of her sister's house, forgetting altogether that there was an elevator.

"It's just idle gossip from journalists who don't know what to write about," Marc answered, glaring at her fiercely. Couldn't she see the kid was in the room?

Alessandro was not that surprised. He knew all about how Germany was dealing with Jews. It upset him, of course. He would much prefer it if his father didn't read the news to him. However, if there was one thing he knew for sure, it was that Italians had nothing, absolutely nothing, in common with the Germans. He listened distractedly to the conversation between his father and Aunt Wanda and Uncle Osvaldo, waiting until it was time to go down into the yard and play with Giamba before it got too dark. The doorman's son was his best friend. They were both ten, and he didn't care that Giamba was still in Elementary School.

"Did you really have to talk about these things in front of the kid?" Marc lashed out at his sister-in-law, more harshly than usual.

"Can't you see she's terrified? She's scared they're going to do here what they're doing in Germany."

Emilia had leaped into the fray, unexpectedly playing the role of defending her sister. "Mussolini and Hitler are good friends," she added, with a sniff of disapproval.

What did Mussolini do after Hitler swallowed Austria up in one gulp, and half an hour later started beating up the Jews? Our *Duce* did nothing. Not a word. Since we all know these things, doesn't a poor little *Jew*-lady from Genoa have the right to be worried?

With Alessandro down in the yard, and no need to protect him any longer, the tension in the room had dissipated. They were merely discussing the news and debating current events as usual. It's what they always did, almost ritually. There was no substance to the articles in the paper. It was plain and simple; just think about it. Were there really too many Jews? Did they actually occupy all the important positions in society? There were the facts: there's one Jew for every 1,000 inhabitants. "Take away the old people, the children, and the women, and how many are left? Where are all these big bosses?" Osvaldo acted nonchalant, as if he didn't care that much.

It was all nonsense: words thrown around to make the headlines. Marc had regained his composure. He regretted having attacked his sister-in-law, but in his view, she had over-reacted. They just had to recall the press campaign in 1934, when there had been insistent reports of a Jewish Anti-fascist plot. It had all blown over, and that had been that. The papers had gone on to the next thing, and the reports had been toned down. Four years had gone by, and the story had become a mere memory.

Luigi had been ready to go out to the *osteria* for ages. They had been talking for too long, and he didn't want to sacrifice his evening. "I can't stand those big fat Fascists," he chimed in, adding his two cents. If they heard his voice, he reckoned, they may remember they were supposed to be going out.

Emilia had other plans, however. She had asked Cesarina to cook for everyone that evening.

"No carafe of wine at our marble table in the *osteria* tonight, no cards. Just talk, talk, talk," Luigi thought to himself. "As if you had the power to change anything with your stupid words."

They soon went back to their normal routine of drinking and cards, however. There had been one more item of news that had caught their attention, but it was a trifling matter: a tiny piece in the paper about far-away Mexico, where the silk workers' union had demanded the immediate expulsion of all the small Jewish businesses in the sector. They had acquired too much power, it seemed. Osvaldo laughed. "What kind of news is that? Who in Italy—or in the whole world, for that matter—had ever heard of those dangerous Mexican Jews in silk pajamas? Who could possibly be interested in a fragment of history of that kind?"

Osvaldo loved taking the stage. He liked everyone to know that he was in the know. He had rushed to the house a few days later to pull out of his sleeve a copy of *Diplomatic Information* that his client always gave him. Mystery solved.

"The Fascist government has no intention of persecuting the Jews," the headline read.

Osvaldo was sitting next to his nephew. There was nothing that might upset him; he just wanted to entertain him. "Look what they do! Instead of printing, for example, the headline 'We don't steal,' they stick in a picture of a thief and they say something like 'We are not like these people.' Poor Mexican silk workers, dragged into this."

"So now we're going to be talking about Mexico, are we?" old Luigi grumbled, looking pleadingly at his sons-in-law to see if they had any intention of going out that evening. He had already donned his hat.

And yet, Mexico was to stay in their minds. Not even twenty days had gone by since that bizarre piece of news had come out. Alessandro was going to the Benvenuto Beach Club every morning, and the radio they had all been waiting for finally arrived. Marc had had to stay in his workshop all night to finish an urgent job for a client who was being transferred.

Osvaldo had been busy delivering little boxes of gaudy jewelry to the lovers of clients whose families were leaving for the summer.

The newspaper had given the *Manifesto of Racist Scientists* pride of place, framed in a box in the middle of the front page. It leapt out with the violence of a stone or a fist shattering a window.

"There is such a thing as the Italian race," the manifesto bellowed to the world, "and Jews do not belong to the Italian race." There were more words that were equally septic. The only population that did not belong in the whole of Italy, it seemed, was the Jewish one.

The splinters of glass continued to fall incessantly on the shadows of Jews trying to protect themselves by covering their heads with their arms. It was as if each and every Jew had been hiding a secret for years, and had just been found out.

Emilia felt a pain in her arm. She supposed she might have caught a cold one day at the beach, when the weather had suddenly changed.

Alessandro was bewildered, sitting there watching and listening to everybody. He was full of regrets. One evening, Aunt Wanda came to the house seeking consolation. She was terrified by some things she'd read in the paper. Alessandro ran down to the yard to play with Giamba, who was waiting for him.

CHAPTER 13

C ome on. Let's think about this for a minute. It's not as if the press has picked up on this idea of the racist manifesto. They're only making a few dry, cautious references to it.

Osvaldo was following his own train of thought, but his tone had changed. He was like a student fumbling for the right answers on a test. If all the huffing and puffing ended up in a cloud of smoke, like last time, the papers would be thrown. Best be cautious, right? The highest circulation Roman daily founded by Mussolini had headlined simply, "An Editorial from *Popolo d'Italia.*" That must be indicative, right? They were just a random combination of words. They were only exploring the question. The "student" had missed a five-line piece in the same paper, however: what had once been called the Demographic Institute under the aegis of the Department of State had been renamed the Demographics and Race Directorate. The transformation had taken place in some obscure little fiefdom of bureaucracy; nobody had taken any notice. Never before had Osvaldo waited so anxiously for the copy of *Diplomatic Information* that his client had always handed over with an air of empty commiseration. Things would finally become clear; the real issues would be explained and revealed.

He arrived at his sister-in-law's house waving the broadsheet as if he were the town crier. "Listen!" he shouted, as he started to read the article out loud. "Many of the impressions gained from abroad regarding Italian racism have been the fruit of a superficial grasp of the facts and of bad faith . . ." Jews should stop complaining. The truth was written right here: "The Fascist government has no special plan to persecute the Jews as such. *Discrimination does not mean persecution.*" Osvaldo recited the final phrase as if he were an actor.

The sisters looked at one another, and when Wanda turned to her husband, she asked him, in a tone that was both adoring and intimidated, "What does that mean?"

"Well," Osvaldo struggled to answer. "It means that if you have guests in your house, you have the right to know who they are and what they do. This doesn't mean you're being hostile towards them."

Marc mimicked a silent clap. With a half-smile on his lips, speaking in a honied tone, he murmured "Bravo! You're right in there with their mentality."

"Explaining something doesn't mean agreeing with it," Osvaldo answered resentfully, accentuating his declamatory style.

"Bravo again! You're even imitating their style of expressing themselves now."

Osvaldo leaped up from his chair in a fury. "Mr. Perfect with your perfect self-control, why on earth can't you ever let me behave like a man from Livorno?"

Marc stared at him. He had no idea what Osvaldo was talking about.

"I mean I'm not allowed to shoot, bang my fists on the table, or give you a punch on the nose if I feel like it."

"Give me a punch, go on. Do it. On condition—for superstition's sake—that it's the only violent thing that will happen to any Jew in the country in the days to come."

"Stop it, already!" Osvaldo said, a little abashed. "You and your stubbornly mild manner. I won't be able to stand you much longer. You just called me a Fascist." Osvaldo rubbed his fist as if he'd actually punched his brother-in-law. Then he smiled and muttered an ancient Jewish proverb to himself: "Rather a slap from a wise man than a kiss from a fool." He was confused, however. He didn't know which category he belonged to.

Emilia glared furiously at her husband, having picked her brother-in-law's side, of course. Alessandro listened on.

Measures against Jews continued to drop on their heads slowly, at irregular intervals, like the first few heavy drops of rain heralding a storm. They found themselves soaked to the bone without realizing they were getting wet. The Laws were being applied before they had even been passed.

The letter on headed paper from the Demographics and Race Directorate was delivered to the Rimon household by a big Carabiniere, who was out of breath after climbing the stairs. Marc took one look at it and dropped into the first chair that happened to be in his path. He sat there in silence, the letter almost falling out of his hand.

"Expulsion," he exclaimed suddenly, breaking the long silence that had already wrapped him in a protective layer. It was only after the family had rushed to his side that he read the second line: "'Foreign citizen entering Italy after 1912.' They're sending me away. They're sending me away!" he started repeating as if he were having an argument with another Marc, who didn't want to understand. He didn't move to his favorite armchair; he was balanced on the edge of the chair as if his seat, his home, his entire existence, had already become precarious.

Then his strength returned. "There are lots of Jews who are worse off than me," he murmured. "People with no citizenship. Nobody will want them. At least I have a British passport." He was frantically striding up and down the room; then he remembered he had to screw a light bulb tight in one of the living-room lamps. He was halfway up the ladder when he heard her scream.

"No!" Emilia was practically clinging to him. "You can't! You can't go! We're a family. We have to stick together."

Marc was stuck there, still as a statue, his arm stretched up towards the ceiling light. He looked as if he were giving a Fascist salute.

"Of course we'll stick together," he said, dumbfounded. "I never thought for one minute I'd leave on my own."

Emilia was already curled up in a corner of the sofa, her arms wrapped around her body and her head bowed. "I'm not leaving. I'm not leaving," she wailed. "Where would my father go? Of course, there's always my sister's place, but I don't want to leave my sister, either . . . and where would we go, anyway? England? I don't know the country. I have no idea what it's like. You always come up with these crackbrained ideas," she snapped. "You're always ready to give up without lifting a finger." There were plenty of influential people who came to his workshop; he could ask them for help. Someone could tear the bloody letter into pieces. If he wasn't prepared to ask his clients, he could at least turn to Osvaldo.

There had been no need for his brother-in-law, in the end. Marc had explained his situation to a dear client, and within a few days the injunction had been annulled. He was tormented by doubt, though. Had he done the right thing?

For Alessandro, it seemed like the meaning of living was opening frightened eyes onto the world. If it had been him, he would have gone to England like a shot. He wouldn't have stopped one minute to think about it.

Marc had told the story of his British passport many times but people tended to forget it; maybe it was too complicated. His father had been born in Belgium and had lived in the Netherlands, but during the Great War he had enrolled as a volunteer in the British Army. He had been a good fighter and had been exposed to mustard gas. By the will of his Majesty's government, he had been awarded a British passport in compensation.

Alessandro loved the austere passport, but his mother didn't want to hear any more talk of England.

A few days later, his parents explained to him, trying to be as blasé as possible, that Jewish children would be banned from every school in the country.

At the end of the summer, he would not be going back to the Eighth-Grade class that waited for him in the narrow alleys near the harbor. Nor would he see his classmates again, the ones who had only recently stopped asking him, "Were you born in Jersualem?"

CHAPTER 14

C arlo, the cousin who was a railway man, wanted to come and see Luigi—that was his excuse, at least. It was clear, however, that he was on a mission to talk to the rest of the family. He had lost his job; they had thrown him off the railways! It was odd: when he had been persecuted as a Communist, they had kept him on, demoting him to work in the warehouses at most. They hadn't fired him. Now, at the bat of an eyelid, he was out for good. Because he was Jewish. Jewish? They knew perfectly well he was a Communist, so how could they believe he had another religion? It was clear and simple. Carlo banged his fists on his forehead as if he were the one who couldn't get his mind around it, not "everyone else."

The same thing happened to the many friends and relatives who were what were known as "Yom Kippur Jews": those who only observed religious strictures on important holidays; religion for them was an indistinct concept, a bygone murmur from a distant past. And yet, there they were, all in the same position. A lugubrious procession of dazed employees who had lost their jobs: clerks, company directors, insurance agents, typesetters, teachers, college professors, army colonels, and delivery boys. Their names had been taken out of the phone books. There were to be no Jewish figures in the newly designed Italian society.

After Carlo the railway man, Adriana's entire family had come to the Rimon house. The cousin who had first discovered

Alessandro could read was now a young woman. They were leaving. They didn't trust a country that was persecuting Jews. The government may well have just been baring its teeth, but for them the first signs were proof enough. Their daughter had been thrown out of school; how was she supposed to carry on her education? They were moving to Latin America where they had some relatives who had provided them with the guarantees they needed to travel.

Was their other "cousin" leaving, too? Alessandro had used their old term of affection for Renata jokingly, trying to disguise his turmoil, but Adriana had rolled her eyes. "Enough with that stupid joke! You know Renata is only Jewish on her paternal grandfather's side." Hadn't the brilliant little kid realized that the script had changed with the times?

Emilia had been unable to hold back. Come on, she had pleaded. Everyone knows they make laws in Italy so they can try them out for a bit and then let them die a quiet death. The laws for Jews were a case in point; they were impossible to enforce in practical terms.

She'd already found a solution for Alessandro's schooling. The nautical academy was immune to politics: it was run by the navy. "They take enrollments from Jews; they don't take a blind bit of notice." Alessandro was listening. This was the first time he'd heard anything about a career as a sailor.

Adriana's family went to sea ten days later, on a boat bound for Argentina.

One evening, Fausto the fugitive's parents—Bruna and Alberto Passigli—arrived unannounced. Bruna's mouth was still painted into a pathetic lipstick heart. They had both aged, but they didn't look overly concerned.

Emilia knew why. Fausto's mother was convinced that, if push came to shove, the unfortunate company her son had been keeping would protect him. The parents would never confess it to anyone, not even to themselves, but there was no doubt that that's what they were thinking. They had come to say hello and find out whether Marc—who was a foreigner, after all—had any news about the merciless persecution that had landed on their heads.

"Information, my foot. I was handed my expulsion papers!" Marc laughed bitterly. "Then they changed their minds," he added hastily, almost in a whisper.

"Ah!" Bruna's expression had lit up. "So, it's true! They do change their minds. It will all fizzle out in the end. Everyone says so," she said, self-righteously.

Between Marc and Osvaldo, there had been no need to clear the air. Marc knew his brother-in-law was no Fascist. He'd never for a second had any doubt. It was simply that Osvaldo liked arguing and often played devil's advocate for the heck of it. The fact that his network of acquaintances granted him access to confidential documents gave him an innocent sense of satisfaction. It was a weakness that he deserved to indulge. The real question was altogether different, but Osvaldo didn't always get it.

Among all the Jews in Italy, Marc was perhaps the best placed of all to pack his bags and leave. He possessed a passport from a powerful nation that was proud to protect its citizens, a job that relied on the skill of his handiwork, which he could take with him to any country, and a portfolio of languages including English. All his brother-in-law needed to do was stop and think for a minute, and he would have understood. Osvaldo should be helping him, urging him to go, but he couldn't do it. All he could think about was how Wanda would take it. How would she ever survive her sister leaving and taking the nephew she considered almost a son away with her?

Was Wanda the only one? Osvaldo set his conscience to

rights every now and again. The Racial Laws might well fizzle out and amount to nothing in the end. Lots of people thought so. Could they really all be wrong?

A meeting. Osvaldo announced the idea as he arrived out of breath at their house one weekday morning. A family meeting. Or rather, a gathering of the whole family—brothers and sisters, children, cousins, cousins of cousins—the entire tribe in a biblical sense. The news had gotten around, and they had grabbed onto it for their lives like drowning castaways gripping a rope. They would be coming from Florence, Milan, Turin, Genoa, Naples, and Rome. The meeting would be held at his brother Sabatino's villa in Livorno, where they would discuss the question of what they should do all together.

"We'll all go, including Alessandro. After all, our ancestors taught us not to sit in judgment alone."

Luigi refused to go. He couldn't stand it as it was, when the four of them blathered on at home. He abhorred the idea of listening to forty of them.

Chapter 15

The villa was white with two square blocks in relief on the facade and a small front garden that was a prelude to the extensive park behind.

Sabatino Nunes ran to the gate to greet his brother. He gave him a hug with one arm, embracing the eleven-year-old Alessandro with the other, even though he'd only ever met him twice. Their host was taller and brawnier than Osvaldo, but decidedly less well dressed. Emilia knew it had nothing to do with his size; her brother-in-law simply had no interest in clothes. His lithe wife Gemma, precisely dressed in white and gray, was like a perpetual reproach.

As soon as they stepped into the house, Marc turned to Gemma, embarrassed. "I know you don't have many guest rooms and that you are intending to put up members of the family here. However, for us . . ."

"Us, what?" Sabatino's forceful physical presence was enough to stop Marc in his tracks.

"It would be fair to reserve the guest rooms for people who can ill afford a hotel or a boarding house. We would be here all day wherever we sleep," Marc murmured.

"You came with my brother!" Sabatino said thunderously. "Your wives are sisters. This house is for the whole family. How could you suggest such a thing?"

Osvaldo had told him how he had sold his brother his share of the villa in order to invest in the jewelry store, but that it hadn't made any difference. Possession has nothing to do with money changing hands. The white villa was inextricably linked to Sabatino, Gemma, their teenage children, and Osvaldo but, most of all to their Polish grandmother, Edith, their progenitor.

When Alessandro had been a child, he'd met her and asked whether she was a queen. She was regal. Like a queen, she never changed; her image was as fixed as a portrait, with her blue eyes and luminous smile. People always said she had never been seen laughing. Or running.

Her matriarchal figure filled the air, endowing the rooms, the blue cushions, the pine trees in the garden with meaning. That day, too, as the guests trickled in, the first thing they all did was run to greet her under the portico in the back garden. One family had brought her a bunch of flowers. Edith clasped them to her breast as if they were the first flowers she had ever received in her life.

Gemma took Wanda and Emilia up to their upstairs guest room. Small apartments or single rooms had been built in the gaps between the trees over the years. In those days, whole families would move in to spend long, scorching-hot summer vacations together by the sea. The women looked down as shadowy figures found their way towards their accommodations in the distance.

Sabatino walked towards the trees with Alessandro and pointed to the clutches of kids his age at the other end of the garden. He could go and join them. Alessandro set off reluctantly. The big man slumped with all his weight into a chair under the portico, next to his brother and brother-in-law.

"Look, look!" he cried, almost in a chant. "Look at all our relatives arriving!" Had they seen their luggage? Hadn't they noticed their suitcases were all the same? How could they have failed to see it? They all contained the same thing: each person's grief was the same as all the others'. "Sure, the kids will start playing together; the women will get reacquainted in no time and make comments on one another's clothes. But there's nothing to be done. We're all in rags." As he spoke, Sabatino pulled at his badly cut shirt, crumpling it even further. "We're already refugees," he said, lowering his voice in order to allow for a hollow laugh. "Refugees in their own country. You're not Italian. You're not Italian," he sang in falsetto, imitating the chirping of a parrot. "They must've had a good dose of imagination to come up with plan like that."

"Stop it!" Osvaldo snapped, leaping out of a chair. "Let's not start! If everything is so clear and inevitable, why are we even meeting? We're here to discuss things, not to have a funeral wake."

"I'd rather be at a funeral," his brother said, staring out at the sky. "There's always someone at a funeral who is there just out of friendship and solidarity. Here that's not the case. There's no one on the sidelines. We're all in the middle of it. It's interesting, isn't it? We're all the same for them. Even the good-looking ones seem like 'ugly louts' to them."

"You're being too pessimistic." Marc, too, was feeling awkward. He had somehow become a victim of the cliché that big men like Sabatino, endowed with superior physical strength, were also more sure of themselves. He had a sudden impulse to divulge his situation—that the authorities had withdrawn his expulsion order—but then he was embarrassed that it had even crossed his mind. It had been a personal favor not a change in government policy. He felt unsettled, over-heated, sweaty.

It was September but the heat was still fierce. Crystal jugs of water with cut fruit, mint leaves and ice had been placed on all the tables in the room and around the garden. Marc drank two glasses in a row. Sabatino kept on drinking, as if he were unable to stop. It looked as though the drink had made him feel better, although there wasn't a drop of alcohol anywhere in sight. "Let's talk about what we've organized for our meeting," he said in a more positive tone.

The plan was to start in the early afternoon that very day and continue throughout Saturday, with a little time on Sunday if it was needed. Anyone could talk for as long as they wanted—there would be no restrictions—but the formal debate would be held in a room that been arranged for the purpose where seats were limited to the heads of each family.

"What about the women?" Marc asked.

Sabatino sighed, exasperated. "The main thing is to choose one person per family, or it will turn into an assembly, a parliament, and we won't be able to decide anything. If one or two of the women decide they want to be present, they can come in and sit down; no one will ask them to leave. It can't be a general rule, though. Miriam, who was an elementary school teacher, for example, had already asked to come. She was unmarried and well educated. Of course, she was welcome."

By four o'clock, all the chairs in the meeting room were occupied: thirty or so people, mostly heads of families, in addition to a couple of men in their forties who were known as successful businessmen but whose family qualities were less well known.

There were very few women. Miriam Sonnino, the teacher, was the object of many a rapid glance. She had wasted the years that were usually spent on getting married catching trains and buses to work in small-town schools up in the mountains. What good had that done her now? She wasn't allowed to teach any more, for the absurd reason that it had suddenly been discovered she was Jewish. A suitor? It was too late for that, and, anyway, everyone in the room was already the "head of a family." Sitting bolt upright on the chair next to her was a thin skeleton of a woman who had arrived from Florence with her husband and son. They all knew that she had inherited from her parents the family business, making large glasses for cognac and fine wines. Her husband, it was rumored, was a little unpredictable, and had erratic interests. That afternoon he had chosen to stay in the garden and keep an eye on the kids.

Leaning on the wall right by the door, Edith presided, meeting people's eyes briefly as they came in. It looked as though she was following every word of the discussion without losing track for a second of what needed to be done in the room: a chair to be brought in, a glass to be changed, new ice to be added to the jugs. Her gestures were measured as she glided around the room; the air didn't even stir.

It was as if a window had been violently blown open by a blast of wind. There were no preliminaries or preparatory speeches. One minute had gone by, and they were already fighting. Those who thought things would *fizzle out* in the end: "Discrimination isn't the same as persecution," pure propaganda would never become reality, it would be too difficult to put these laws into practice, bits of the law will fall by the wayside until sooner or later there will be nothing left to speak of. "What are you talking about?" the other side yelled. "Can't you see what's happening in Germany and Austria? Are you blind?" There was only one choice: leave. Get away while they still could. The raised hands looked more like threats than requests to speak.

Sabatino left the room. Some people wondered whether the tone of the debate hadn't become too heated—insults had been bandied about. Might their host have been offended in his own house? He came back a few minutes later in a white shirt, coat, and tie, and with a minimal gesture asked to speak.

"It's Friday evening," he said. "It's time for *Kabbalat Shabbat*, the Sabbath Welcome. As everyone's jaws dropped, he explained that in the little room at the end of the corridor, his mother had lit the Sabbath candles, and the more observant members of the gathering had already moved there to say their prayers. "I invite anyone who would like to participate to come."

Silence fell in the room. At the back, there were a few die-hards who were still arguing in angry hushed tones. "I'm going," Sabatino announced. The silence grew even deeper. At that point, almost against their will, three people rose from their chairs.

CHAPTER 16

Less than ten minutes later, Sabatino stormed back into the room.

"Aren't you coming to prayers?" he asked his brother.

"What, me?" Osvaldo answered, trying to sound disinterested. "I was actually wondering why you were going. We've never been religious."

"I'm the host here, and some of our relatives are." Sabatino's tone was gearing up to a whine. "What am I supposed to do? Let them go and pray on their own?" Then he clumsily added, as if he were translating from another language for his brother's benefit, "Do you realize they don't even have enough men to form a *minyan*."

He then felt obliged to remind the members of the family who claimed not to be religious that the quorum for Jewish prayer is ten males over thirteen years of age. His words were aimed directly at Osvaldo. "You're my brother, so you're the host, too. It's about good manners, and respect."

"I don't think it's respectful to take part in a ritual you don't believe in."

"You go to synagogue at Yom Kippur, don't you? And you don't eat pork at home, right?"

"Those are traditions, old family customs. Do you remember when they used to take us all to Great-Aunt Carola's for her birthday and she always made the same apple fritters?"

"You can tell it however you like," Sabatino cut in, his tone sharp as a razor. "Do you really think this is the time to harp on about our *visits to Great-Aunt Carola*?"

Neither of them made a move. Osvaldo stared at Marc, but Marc refused to meet his gaze. Sabatino felt he was losing the battle. "What about you?" he said, turning to Marc resentfully. "If you take part in a blessing, do you feel you're violating your secular spirit or your internationalism?"

Marc had not traveled from Genoa to Livorno with all his family to engage in age-old provocations of the kind.

Sabatino looked sheepish. He muttered that they shouldn't carry on the conversation while some people had taken half an hour off to pray. They were sidelining them, that's what they were doing. The word "sidelining" seemed to do the trick. Osvaldo and Marc started making their way to the communal prayer room, followed in dribs and drabs by almost all the others, until the room was practically empty.

Sabatino looked pleased. He had won this particular battle, but he spent the entire evening wondering why he had bothered.

In the light of the Shabbat candles, Marc saw his wife holding the old *tefillah* wrapped in a flowery-patterned cloth. Her sister, wearing a pearl necklace, was by her side, and they were surrounded by a group of women already immersed in their prayers. Towards the back of the room, wearing a borrowed *kippah* that was too big for his head, stood Alessandro. He wasn't even old enough to make up the *minyan*; why on earth hadn't his mother left him to his own devices?

The men filed into the room, as if they were being guided without even knowing it. A muddled outer circle was beginning to form around those already involved in the *Kabbalat Shabbat*. Displaying a whole range of attitudes, they slowly started picking up fragments of words and notes. These ancient fragments—from who knows where and when—had been with them forever, and just then they were gripped, oblivious for an instant to the outside world. As they came back to their senses, however, they were uneasy, well aware that their problems couldn't be solved by abandoning themselves to flights of fancy.

Circling outwards, almost to the edges of the room as if to stress they were only there as a courtesy, were the ranks who did not identify with any religion and who considered themselves open-minded universalists. Italians, in short, who were indistinguishable, in terms of their frameworks and beliefs, from every other Italian who was the product of the Risorgimento and the Great War. There were some older men, on the other hand, who—either out of sheer exuberance of character or extreme self-confidence—were momentarily lulled into joining the chorus or chanting a verse of a Jewish blessing they had culled from nowhere.

When it came to the *Lekhah Dodi*, "Let's go, my beloved, to meet the bride, and let us welcome the presence of Shabbat," the circles merged confusedly into one another as the entire congregation turned together. Then *Kabbalat Shabbat* was brought to a close.

In the corridor, on their way back to the meeting, Marc spoke urgently to Osvaldo. With everything that was going on, and all the uncertainty regarding his future education, pulling Alessandro this way and that for no reason was unnecessary. Dragging him to a religious ceremony he couldn't understand was one more way to confuse him.

"Welcome among us." A slightly shrill voice from behind them came from a pale-faced young man with a scraggly beard, wearing a black *kippah*. It took Osvaldo a few seconds to recognize him: Michele, a distant relative who had been studying to be a rabbi. Was he welcoming Osvaldo, who was, after all, one of the hosts?

"Here we are, citizens of the world," the young man went on unperturbed. "You have no desire to sit alongside those of us who do not shave our beards," he said, alternating his glance between Osvaldo and Marc. His smile was anything but friendly.

Osvaldo didn't answer. It was clear that the young lad had written his little speech in advance and would decide at the last minute who to address.

"When you come to fill in the accursed census form, in the space where you are asked to specify your religion, you can try writing 'agnostic', or free-thinker, disciple of Bakunin or Jove. For them, whatever you write will translate the same as for those of us who recite the *Shema* twice a day: Jewish race."

Enough! Who did the youth with the scraggly beard they had run into in the corridor think he was? Osvaldo was unable to contain his fury. Earlier, in the garden, his brother had said something similar but no, no, no. This was not the spirit. His brother had waxed philosophical, but his spirit had been generous. Admittedly, he had shown off a little but he had not made up his mind yet which side to take. That apprentice rabbi Michele had ruined everything with the usual spiel about how waylaid Jews need to return to the fold.

"Stop it, Michele. This is not the way to behave," another voice called out, the man's father or teacher, perhaps. "'You cannot teach if you are consumed by anger.' You remember Hillel's teachings, don't you?" the gentle voice coaxed.

Michele looked bewildered. He stood stock still, all of a sudden confused and anxious.

His eyes were baby-blue. Osvaldo observed him at length and finally decided he rather liked the young Michele, who was trembling with passionate indignation.

The man who had spoken to him linked arms with him and slid out of the room murmuring, "Sorry, sorry," as they left.

"They're young. They don't accept things," Marc said,

thinking of Alessandro whenever he crossed his arms looking hostile.

In the big room looking out onto the garden, a woman in a blue dress with big buttons arranged diagonally across it, as if they were an admiral's sash, ran after young Michele's teacher. "Excuse me, Rebbe?" she called, a little out of breath. "Given the danger, what about converting temporarily to Christianity, like the Marranos did? They went back to being Jews when they were allowed to."

"'When you are drowning, grabbing onto a sword won't keep you afloat.'"

Was Rebbe's smile reproachful or sympathetic? The woman was unsure. So were Osvaldo and Marc.

CHAPTER 17

Once, when Alessandro was a child, his parents had taken him to the theater. Aunt Wanda and Uncle Osvaldo had come along, too. Some friends acted in an amateur drama group and they wanted to support them. Alessandro had been unable to follow the plot, because he hadn't been able to stop staring at a thin, balding actor attempting to play his part. The man had managed to get his words out alright, but his arms . . . his arms looked like annoying appendages pinned onto his body; the character appeared to have no connection with them at all. He had no idea where to put them. He waved them about as if he had been trying to bat off an insect glued to his sleeve. What if something like that happens to me? Alessandro had thought, scared out of his wits. What if I end up looking at a part of my body as if it didn't belong to me?

Now it was no longer his arms but his whole body, from his forehead to the tips of his toes. He felt superfluous, in the way, shapeless. He had walked to the end of the garden in vain; he had even wandered through the corridors of the house, giving one of the waitresses a fright. Nobody even cared who he was. He knew he should go up to one of the other kids and say, "Hey," "What's your name?" or something like that—like when he was at nursery school—but he couldn't face it. Then his mother had dragged him into the middle of a religious ceremony, but he hadn't been able to follow a thing and noticed his father had looked equally lost.

The following day, the debate in the living room was more heated from the start than it had been the evening before, when it had been interrupted so brusquely. The religious members of the family had mingled amongst the others after their prayers. He couldn't go in; he knew that much.

The only thing left for him was to try and find a purpose to his wandering. In the middle of the back garden there was a man-made pool shaped like a Venetian gondola. It was dry; they must have been restoring it. There were empty barrels all around the edges, old rusty buckets, and rolled up lengths of rope. A group of kids had taken it over: the game was to drop themselves down into its depths and then attempt to climb out again by taking a running jump. If that didn't work out, they grabbed onto the ropes held taut for their benefit by their guffawing companions.

Alessandro jumped in and was able to get out easily. He had been quick and agile and had never even considered using the rope. He had always been good at gymnastics. He realized the others had been impressed and repeated the feat three times, the third just to give them satisfaction. He'd done it already so why bother repeating it?

The kids helped a younger girl drop down into the depths and then strained to pull her up as she gripped onto the rope. The little girl kicked and shrieked, seemingly as happy as punch. Alessandro had thrown himself onto the grass. The slanting sun-rays and a sea breeze were reason enough to at least attempt to be happy.

A blond boy came and sat next to him. He had noticed before that he was being friendly. The first thing he asked was where Alessandro came from. It was a logical question, given that the sad cast of characters gathered in the villa came from so many different cities. Genoa? What a coincidence. His family was planning to move there because a big town was better for Jews at the moment, what with the school situation and everything. How old was he? Eleven, same as him. Had he done the Elementary School exam? "I'm in Seventh Grade," Alessandro had answered, as usual almost in a whisper. The boy stared at him, more annoyed than admiring. His sister was at the other end of the gravel path sitting under a palm tree. "You're in the same class; why don't you go and talk to her, instead. You may end up in the same school." His voice had become aggressive, almost hostile.

Under the palm tree. Black curly hair and deep-set eyes, as attractive as Jole, the woman his cousin Fausto had eloped with. He couldn't utter a word. He stared at the girl, dumbstruck. "Are you coming, Alma?" a boy called out to her.

"Are you coming, Alma?" He heard the words as if they were an echo. Alma. It was just right. She had been given the perfect name: beauty that saves the soul. Then he suddenly dropped back to earth. He was from Genoa, yes, he was eleven like her brother, and he was supposed to be going into Eighth Grade.

"I've got news for you!" Alma shouted to the friend who had been calling her. "This kid is going to be in our class!" The other boy didn't hear.

Alma smiled. Her smile was kind, protective, but not flirtatious.

"Let's go to the beach," another boy said. He was tall, thick-set, with bristly hair that had clearly been attacked with a wet brush but was still sticking up all over his head like the pencils in the ad on the billboards.

The beach? Alma was unsure. Weren't Jews banned? "Come on, they'll only know the local Jews. They won't know anything about Jews from out of town. How will they be able to tell?" He started to tug at her arm, laughing.

"I won't be in Eighth Grade at a Jewish school with you," Alessandro blurted out as he followed Alma. "My mother has found out that the nautical academy takes Jews. They don't take any notice; all they care about is the sea."

"The nautical academy?" the bristly boy teased. "You Genoese are always making up stories!" He turned to an imaginary audience on the lawn under the trees and bowed. "Ladies and gentlemen, let me introduce a future little sailor!"

"Do you want to come to the beach with me?" Alma murmured, looking uneasy.

"No, I need to go and buy a newspaper for my father."

Neither of them was listening.

The door of the meeting room was not closed. Marc saw his son lurking outside and went to see what was wrong with him. He asked for some money so that he could go buy the newspaper and *L'avventuroso*, his weekly magazine. His father was relieved.

Alessandro went the long way around to the newsagents. He was on his own and could do what he wanted. There was never anybody to keep him company. Nobody likes me. I never say the things I'm supposed to say; I don't even know what I'm supposed to say. If I did, I could at least pretend. I run a mile before I'm rejected. That way I always win. What a genius. All that stuff about being too old or too young is just an excuse. That's all it is. Let's be honest here, at least to ourselves. Maybe this is what being Jewish means? You are the one seeking others and then escaping, while they accept you and then reject you. He felt different, awkward, not only about his age or school work, but about everything, everywhere, from top to toe, in every aspect of his existence, even wearing the Genoa soccer-team jersey he had insisted on putting on before going out. Playing the Jew among Jews . . . now that required a certain degree of imagination.

He sat at the edge of the lawn, leaning on a side wall of the villa. The windows of the meeting room were wide open and from where he was, he could clearly hear every word the adults were saying, including the insults and sighs.

Alessandro opened the copy of *L'Osservatore Romano* he had bought for his father and started reading. He doggedly made his way through the articles, almost flaunting the fact that he was reading a newspaper. He would have liked someone to notice and be amazed, but there was hardly anyone on that narrow strip of lawn. He thought he saw his mother in the distance, but he may have been wrong.

He was no longer reading the paper; he had started listening.

Would all those brothers, uncles, and cousins, wise men and cowards, know-it-alls and incurable optimists work out how to save the Italian Jews?

CHAPTER 18

He listened. The words billowed out of the room in great gusts and dispersed in the mild air of the garden. He was the only one there who could catch them. Sitting against a wall, completely still, covered by a newspaper that rendered him invisible, only he could give meaning to those words.

Evian. He'd never heard of the place before. His father had never spoken about Evian. In July, less than two months before—he was able to make out—that was where the leaders from almost all the important countries had met in order to try to save the Jews in Germany and Austria. They had asked which countries were willing to take them in. "Guess who answered?" The voice of the person speaking, though slightly nasal, sounded harsh and aggressive. He sounded like a young lawyer pleased by his closing arguments. "No one. That's who answered," he concluded, dropping his voice a tone. The thirty-two countries gathered in Evian had agreed to increase their quota of immigrants by practically nothing; it was laughable. They were throwing small change at them, whatever they had in the left pockets of their pants. As for the United States? They'd been the ones to call the meeting. They had raised their quota a little bit, but within the portion already reserved for Germans. Were the Jews who were trying to escape the country supposed to sit on the same benches on the same ship as their (probable) persecutors? Someone had shouted this—or maybe they hadn't? Alessandro wasn't entirely sure he hadn't shouted it inside himself. The wall behind him was no longer simply support; it was protection. No, it was a trench. They may have already started shooting from the back of the garden.

Now they were talking about Switzerland. What about the country everyone knew was the "land of refuge"? Seemingly this was no longer true. Switzerland had asked the Austrians to stamp a J on Jewish passports. They felt they had the right to know who was knocking at their door. They certainly had no intention of becoming a "country for Jews." The word "neutrality" had a precise meaning that shouldn't be overlooked. The observations and accusations bandied about in the family gathering were now chaotic fragments.

"So," a woman, almost certainly Miss Sonnino, the teacher, yelled. "Where's the sense in all their talk about us leaving the country if there's not one pitiful nation that welcomes Jews? You've brought us here to mock us." It's the other way around, people rushed to correct her from a different place in the room. The German and Austrian Jews are trapped now. They should have left earlier, when it was hard but still possible. That's why we're here today.

"Dragged out of their beds at night." A voice with a strong foreign accent had suddenly joined in the chorus, as if he were chanting a dirge or a prayer. "Torn away from their homes, tortured, humiliated, ransacked, everything from their candlesticks to their families taken away from them. And all the while they were laughing. Laughing at us." There could have been an "Amen" after every word he uttered but the chanting dissolved into a chilling bark of a laugh.

Alessandro grabbed hold of the newspaper, trying desperately to read something—anything—rather than listen.

However, in the wake of the man's abrupt silence, the "reasonable" people were able to chime in. Come on, you know things will be different in Italy. They'll never be able to enforce the Racial Laws. They'll fall by the wayside, just you wait and see. Italians aren't racist, it's just that they don't want any trouble. Protesting is hard, and right now it's dangerous.

Brief snippets cut across the room, overlaying one another. Everyone was trying to say something, but nobody was listening.

"I'd like to make a proposal." Alessandro recognized the voice that had risen over the hubbub in the room. It belonged to one of the successful businessmen. "Let's create a family fund for those who want to leave. People with more money can help those with less." The room filled with chatter: relief, embarrassment, and the burden of gratitude. The conversation was no longer one; it had broken up into little groups. Alessandro was unable to follow.

He was still sitting against the wall under the window. The beautiful Alma and the bristly boy were walking towards him.

"Didn't you go to the beach?" he asked, taking the initiative.

"We saw someone who knew me. It wasn't worth trying," the boy blustered. He glanced up at the window. "What are you doing here? Spying?" Alessandro shook his head. "No. I already know everything they're saying."

The two of them walked off, chattering to each other. Neither of them was laughing at him.

At lunch time, he looked for his parents. In the garden and under the porticoes, long trestle tables had been set out for a buffet-style meal. The observant Jews were comfortably seated in their full regalia at a table of their own. Marc was worried about his son. He had hoped he wouldn't still be on his own, that he would have found a friend among so many kids. "He feels a little superior to the others," his wife said, reading his mind.

The debate started again after lunch. Alessandro wanted to

go on eavesdropping, but not from the lawn because he knew they would close the windows at sundown.

He crept into the antechamber and saw that the doors of the living room were wide open. He could even see some of the participants in the distance, including Nonna Edith, as stiff as a ramrod, sitting in the last row looking like royalty. She had seen him and caught his eye for a second. Did that mean he could stay? He sat on a wooden chest. If he managed to sit still among all the vases and marble busts, they might take him for a statue.

They were talking about the census now. Almost all of them had misunderstood the issue. It wasn't a real census, like the one administered to the whole Italian population. It was a separate enquiry put together by the new Minister for Race, aimed exclusively at Jews. It wasn't statistics. It was po-li-tics! Racial politics, of course.

"The form only requires you to state your religion. It doesn't mention race," a short and shy man with a crown of thinning hair surrounded by a bald pate stammered.

The big man who stood up to answer was destined to win the argument on size alone. "Read it properly," he said, using the familiar "tu" in order to diminish his opponent further. "Read the ministry form properly. It's called Register of Residents of Jewish Race. You can write the little word 'Jewish' under the heading Religion but it will jump right out again and bounce back into its correct position under Race!"

Alessandro was watching a young man with blue eyes who seemed to be turning towards his father and staring at him. It might have been accidental. They didn't know the guy.

They were arguing. Quick decisions were of the essence this time around; they had already missed the deadline for the census. Well, they had all waited for the family meeting before filling the thing in. There was no consensus, however. I'm throwing the form in the garbage can; if we hand it in, we'll just be giving them an excuse to persecute us; I'll just write "Jewish", they know anyway; but if someone doesn't complete the form there'll be serious trouble . . .

Alessandro looked on. He didn't know what he would have chosen to do. He was reminded of Nonno Luigi's proverb: "Better a living dog than a dead lion." He said it a lot. Nonna must have taught him the expression before she left her grandson the gold chain. That must mean it was a Jewish proverb.

One evening, once they were back home, every one of those honest citizens would fill in that form, in the light of the table lamp, following all the rules as closely and carefully as they had done when they did their class work under the teacher's watchful eye.

The Sabbath was drawing to a close, as was the debate. It had melted down into a thousand rivulets waiting for the new impulses the following day would bring. The tide of people flowed out of the room into the corridors and vestibules, mingling with the women and children. Now that the restrictions imposed on them by the Sabbath had been lifted, the observant Jews—who had contributed to the debate with such fervor—were scribbling feverishly on sheets of paper folded into four, writing sloping lists of names and addresses and searching for the fundraising list so they could sign up.

There was no joy in that family gathering, only the heat generated by their physical proximity.

"I saw you, you know, behind the door of the antechamber," Alessandro's father said. "Did you listen to the whole thing?"

"I wasn't behind the door," Alessandro answered, before wandering off.

He was happier watching them from a distance. His father and Uncle Osvaldo were joined at the hip, firing off answers to questions in all directions as if they had one body with two heads.

A pale, scruffy man Alessandro recognized approached them. He used to come to their house once or twice a year; now he was pushing his way past the crowds heading straight for them.

Marc took a second to clock who he was. Ruggero Coen was from Milan; somebody must have paid his train fare. He would come to Genoa every now and again looking for friendship in the form of a loan. The young man, who looked old before his time, had great imagination; his head was always swilling with ideas. Business was always bad, and it was always due to some unexpected misfortune.

"Nice villa, eh?" he said, trying to get them on his side any way possible. At their automatic "yes," he felt he had gained a sufficient footing and launched right into his plea. He was going through a difficult period and urgently, urgently needed help.

"Weren't you listening? We've just decided to set up a solidarity fund, which you will be able to dip into I'm sure," Marc answered with straightforward sincerity.

Ruggero, meanwhile, had set his sights on Osvaldo. "I have no intention of leaving. I need money straight away. I need to get my things in order right now . . . otherwise I'm in danger. I'll tell you later."

Marc and Osvaldo knew the kinds of things he was talking about; they were always the same with him. This was not the time for the usual kind of help, though. Everything was going into one pot; that way many, many more Jews could be saved. Osvaldo was on the team organizing the fundraiser. Marc would join, too . . . He was not the type to be cruel in order to be fair, but this time it was called for. Saying no to Ruggero saddened them both deeply.

Alessandro had followed the exchange from a distance. He'd just started to approach them when he saw the lady he used to call "the queen" walking towards them from the other side of the room. The queen, in her usual polite way, was beckoning the man from Milan who had been confabulating with his father and Uncle Osvaldo.

"Please excuse me," she said. "I just happened to hear what you were asking our relatives here. If you will allow me, I'd like to help you myself." The envelope she slipped into Ruggero Coen's hand must have been prepared beforehand.

"Thank you, thank you," Ruggero muttered, confused. He had glimpsed the outline of a cheque inside. His eyes flashed. There may have been a tear or two.

"No, I must be the one to thank you. You gave me the opportunity to do a *mitzvah*," the old matriarch said, gliding away in her regal fashion.

CHAPTER 19

They were on their own in the train. Osvaldo and Wanda had decided to stay a few more days in Livorno. The glass door of the compartment, tightly closed, felt almost laughably like the only protective barrier life was able to offer them at that moment.

Alessandro sat in silence, caught up in his thoughts. Marc would have given anything to know what they were. As it turned out, he didn't have to wait long.

I'm not a genius. I'm not a genius . . . Alessandro said to himself over and over in a singsong voice, like a chant set to the beat of the rocking train. He had never thought of himself as a genius. He knew he was a good student, a little precocious perhaps. He also knew that his mother and close relatives were the only ones who were ecstatic about it; he annoyed practically everybody else. Why should people bother to make the effort to understand him, anyway?

He felt as though his senses had been awakened, there was a glimpse of possibility, even though the world had become increasingly indifferent to him. There was one thing that he was absolutely sure about; it was no more than a spark of an idea before, but now it was charged with a sharp electric energy.

He was eleven, and until then he had always felt like Samuel in the Bible, *the one who listens*. He had been listening to adults arguing for months. In the past few days in the white villa he had seen them pick fights, contradict one another, tussle, cling onto the most charismatic among them, pretend to listen all the time wishing the speaker would stop talking so they could give their own opinion. He had recognized those who were so anxious they could not put their thoughts into words, and those fatalists who thought a smile and a positive outlook would keep them on the right side of destiny . . .

He had understood everything. They had put him on a pedestal as a child when there was no reason for it. Now, with true modesty, apologizing a thousand times a day, he knew exactly what needed to be done. The Italian Jews had to leave.

"We have to go, at least those of us who can," he said for the first time on that train, gazing up at his mother and father after a long silence. His tone was light, as if he were saying something entirely predictable that only needed to be translated into practical terms.

His mother made her usual sour face; she narrowed her eyes and pursed her lips. "Here is our great big know-it-all who wasn't able to find anyone good enough for him during our whole stay."

His father stopped her with a mild, "Let's listen to what he has to say!" but Emilia had already raised the stakes.

"You're no genius!" she yelled. "We even had to pay for extra private lessons this year!"

Alessandro stood up and pulled his little suitcase down from the luggage rack. He had packed the copy of *L'Osservatore Romano* that his father had left in the garden. It was the first thing that popped out when he flipped the clasps open. He lifted the newspaper, ignoring it completely, and pulled out his comic, *L'avventuroso,* stuck his nose into it, and read for the rest of the journey.

His parents were speaking quietly. The suppressed, unexploded argument made the atmosphere unbearable. Leave. It was a theoretical concept, a random squiggle of a pencil on a scrap of paper. What about the important things in life: family, money, language? You look up at a different sky and tell yourself, "There's no Fascism here," but is that enough? Marc said yes, it is. I've lived in many different countries. It's possible. You'd jump into a freezing river if they were chasing you down.

Alessandro clasped his hands behind his neck, pulling down hard so that there would be no way he could lift his head out of his comic book.

Osvaldo and Wanda returned to Genoa a few days later. Osvaldo did not really know whether his nephew had enjoyed the trip to Livorno; he had seemed a little lost. Emilia had told her brother-in-law about the obsession the boy had developed with leaving the country. Someone must have scared him there.

Uncle Osvaldo asked Alessandro if he wanted to go and get gelato at their favorite café. As they walked, even the thorniest topics—channeled into their normal way of communicating—were smoothed down into everyday subjects. The new anti-Jewish campaign promoted by the Fascists? Uncle Osvaldo's smile was more skeptical than bitter. Let's see how things go. He wasn't pessimistic. He could see other people's point of view—of course he could—but he had no intention of leaving. He would throw himself into the fundraiser for any relatives who wanted to go but couldn't afford it. "You see what we can do in a religion without dogma?"

Alessandro stared at his uncle. He'd never heard him talk about religion before. He took regular steps so that he could talk more easily. Lots of people knew Osvaldo. They stopped and greeted him. Nobody was as smooth a talker as he was.

The old-fashioned café they were now sitting at seemed to have been designed with a customer like him in mind. Uncle and nephew sat side by side and ordered the same cup of chocolate gelato they always went for.

Alessandro looked around, filled with curiosity. At the table next to theirs, there were two middle-aged men talking about this and that, jumping from one subject to another, in order to pass the time of day from the sound of it. At one point, he clearly heard the word "Jew." They had said something like, "The *Duce* has put these Jews in their place." "And it was about time," they added, then laughed and moved on to the next thing. Uncle Osvaldo must have heard, too. Alessandro fired a rapid glance at him, but his face was flat, almost without any expression. That's how elegant folk behave.

What happened next was like a movie. His uncle slowly got to his feet and then, with a lightning quick movement, lifted the marble-topped table and flipped it unceremoniously over the two unsuspecting customers. The chairs went flying, and the cups, still filled with coffee, rolled onto the ground alongside the little pastry dishes. The two men were staggering to their feet, dazed and scared. The owner of the café was dusting down their jackets with ineffectual little pats. He turned to the other customers, attempting to reassure them with his gestures, while he resolutely pushed uncle and nephew out onto the street.

Alessandro stood outside on the sidewalk and stared. He never ceased to be amazed by his uncle, who was already setting off with the same lackadaisical pace as ever. "Don't forget, I'm from Livorno," was all he said.

CHAPTER 20

H e didn't feel left out at the naval academy. Nobody was mean to him or asked him whether he was born in Jerusalem. They hardly noticed him. A younger kid in the third course, who had nothing in common with the interests and methods of the establishment, was a mystery and at the same time completely irrelevant, not even worth investigating. His enrollment there must have been a mistake. The mistake was soon ironed out by the head teacher, who called Alessandro's parents in to his office less than ten days later. He was a man of another era, educated to display good manners at all times. He was terribly sorry, there had been a misunderstanding, it was the law, the Jewish boy could not possibly stay . . .

The only alternative was Jewish school. Classes were held in private homes with long tables set up in big rooms. Real classrooms would be ready soon; the workmen were rushing to complete an extra floor above the synagogue.

Alessandro tried not to think about it too much. He loved surprises, and in his mind there was one scene in particular that he replayed: bumping into Alma. She would, of course, pretend she had forgotten him. And then, one day, there she was in flesh and blood, sitting at the walnut dining table of the Sacerdotis' house. He almost jumped out of his skin. She looked like one of those naive, slightly childish saint's cards they give out in front of the church. God, or someone who was working under his orders, must have played his part, because the only ray of sunlight coming through the window was shining on her and her alone. The others were part of the furniture, indistinguishable from the long wooden bench that served as a collective school desk. They were bent over their books at a table that clearly belonged in a private home, but the teachers' lack of indulgence soon reminded them that this was a school.

"What happened to the naval academy?" Alma whispered to him. Alessandro shrugged. She smiled almost as if he were her "equal."

At the end of the lessons, Alessandro slipped out of the classroom in a hurry. Without even knowing why, his legs were taking him to his old school in the narrow alleyways of the city center. He wasn't planning on seeking anyone out or calling out to one of his former schoolmates. He didn't go to the gate. The other side of the street was close enough. A chance throw of the dice would decide his destiny. Someone was bound to see him. Even though they had teased him in the first year, they were still his friends. He was no longer a victim of their incessant teasing.

They came out in small groups. They were hardly speaking to one another, staring at the ground or straight ahead. He watched their backs and heavy satchels as they walked away. The sky was muffled and gray.

When he got home, Giamba was already in the courtyard. "Didn't you go to school today?" Alessandro yelled. Couldn't he see he had a cold? Alessandro was clutching his trading cards of famous cyclists, and his friend pulled his own cards out of his pocket. Nothing in the world could touch their little corner of the yard.

When his mother was angry, she never showed it. This time, he noticed, she was making a huge effort to control herself. "They came to take our radio away," she said in the same tone she would use to tell a joke. With a subtle change of timbre, she went on to reveal that it had been the police. She gave up pretending all was well, fuming because he hadn't even asked why. So, he thought he knew everything, did he? It was one of the new laws against Jews, she told him, but she also wanted him to know that they had confiscated radios from some families but then given them back. Marc poked his head through the door of his laboratory but went straight back to work. It was nothing.

When they had to send Cesarina away, Emilia didn't hold up so well. She wandered in and out of the kitchen looking lost, every now and again directing an angry scowl at her husband. Who would help her with the housework now? To make matters worse, Matilde, Cesarina's mother, had descended on them straight from their rural village and was shaking the poor girl by the shoulders yelling, "What have you done, you wretched girl? You may as well confess right now. Getting yourself fired like this!" Marc tried to explain that it was the law. Jews were no longer allowed to employ Aryan domestics. What are Jews? Are they enemies of Fascism, like Communists? Not really; well, a little, perhaps. Marc was running out of answers. "Well, in that case," Matilde said in a huff, "we're the ones who are choosing to go." She rudely grabbed the fold of bills that the "master of the house" had laid out on the table and, even more rudely, tugged at her daughter, who was, in her turn, gripping onto her suitcase. "It's not what you think," the girl wailed. "They're all good people here in Rome." She managed to free herself from her mother's hold and ran towards Emilia, lunging into an awkward embrace. Mrs. Rimon told her off every now and again, for sure, but she took good care of her and on Sundays always said, "Wash the dishes quickly and then you can go out for a lovely walk."

As soon as the classrooms above the synagogue were ready,

school went back to normal. There were desks, a table for the teacher, a janitor, and a bell ringing at the end of the lessons. The teachers were the same, but once they returned to a real school they went back to their old ways. Alma and he had become friends. She was very different from the blonde girl with the carefully styled hair he had first met. There was no need for her to suck up to him to get help on her tests. She was actually better than him. Their class essays vied for top marks; being competitive, in its turn, made them even more creative. There were times when coming second had a more complex, nuanced flavor than the vaguer taste of triumph. Both Alessandro and Alma picked up on things that had never been said, often simultaneously.

The boy with the bristly hair Alessandro had met in Livorno was now in their class. His name was Sergio Segre. He nearly always left school with Alma, and they chatted companionably. They'd known one another for years, since long before Alessandro had come along. Sergio was pretty bad at Latin and Italian. Alessandro thought (or wished he thought) that you couldn't be jealous of someone who has nothing in common with you. His and Sergio's hopes and dreams would always be on parallel paths. They went roller-skating with other school friends at the Albaro Lido. Jews were not allowed to be there, but they didn't exactly have the word "Jew" printed on their foreheads. They raced along the track in formation, as light as a flock of swallows in flight. Stay together, be prepared to disband or defend the others "if anything happens." This was their instinct, though they would never put it into words. Being a group was not such a bad thing. Mussolini clearly hadn't thought things through when he banned them from going to school. Rabbi Bonfiglioli often joked, "It's not great being alone even in Paradise." He didn't want any sad-looking Jewish kids around. Every Sunday he made sure a little party would be held in one Jewish household or another, conducted under his suavely imperious baton. Cake, orangeade, and music. Dancing was a matter of age: being thirteen or over gave you access to the starting line. Alessandro's job was to wind up the gramophone. When he put on Fedora Mingarelli's hit, "Un'ora sola ti vorrei," some of the parents smiled. He knew they were thinking of Mussolini's fat imperial face.

Alessandro was surprised to find himself gesticulating with his arms like those old men who talk to themselves in their empty houses. He admitted he may even have talked to himself sometimes after thinking too hard. He was uncomfortable in his skin. He found it difficult to put his feelings and ideas in order. Was it possible that his life was actually going quite well at the moment?

He was going to a new school, Alma was there, the other kids were on speaking terms with him, they all did their homework together and went roller-skating afterwards, and there was always his childhood gang to fall back on in the courtyard. His father was working as hard as ever; they seemed to have forgotten to take his license away. His clients wouldn't have cared anyway. Whether he was a Jew or not, they would still require his services. They would still take him their diamonds to restore. Sure, they had confiscated their radio, but they'd had it for such a short time they'd hardly had a change to get used to it. Their home help, Cesarina, had had to go, but that just meant one person fewer for his mother to get in a mood with. She still moaned all the time, but she was less shrill about it. It was easy to shut her out. Could it be that he—that the whole family—had adapted?

His life felt like a derailed train that was still running off the tracks. The ground was treacherous, dangerous, full of potholes, but it was, nonetheless, firm ground and therefore somehow reassuring. Was the human urge to give up really that strong? Things that only yesterday might have seemed unbearable, today were easy to swallow without any effort at all.

On New Year's Eve, Nonno Luigi quipped, "Aren't we raising a glass tonight?"

"What's to celebrate?" his daughter complained.

"If only we could go back in time . . ." Marc murmured. "If we could go back to '37!"

Alessandro kept his mouth shut, thinking of the rickety train rumbling along without any tracks.

"Well, I'm alive," Luigi said leaping out of his chair. "Ask that rabbi of yours." Alessandro knew he would come out with the phrase; the whole family was resigned to hearing him say it at every opportunity. "Ask him whether he's ever seen the words 'better a living dog than a dead lion.'" The fact that he was a living dog meant that he at least—the others could do what they liked—but at least he would drink a glass of wine to celebrate the beginning of 1939, though he knew perfectly well it was not shaping up to be a favorable year for them.

CHAPTER 21

Lelio was friends with the whole family; he could turn up any time at their home. This time it was a frosty early morning visit.

"The Austrian Jews," he said. He was out of breath, almost feverish. "They're pouring into Italy by the thousands."

Yes, they were the last desperate attempts. The trapdoors were already closing. It was already a tragedy. None of the countries—not even the ones that had met a few months before to draw up a plan—were willing to take the poor refugees in.

"Only Italy," he muttered, as if he were talking to himself.

"Italy? But Italy is an ally of the Third Reich!" Marc exclaimed. It was unusual for him to be surprised by anything.

"There's nothing official. You know how these things go: one eye shut and the other looking the other way. Lots of people too stupid to notice, and one, plus one, plus one more person finding creative solutions. Does that explain it?" Lelio smiled, like in the old days. For a minute or two.

The flocks of Jews who had managed to escape from Austria were all arriving in Genoa. This was why a committee had been formed.[2] Lelio was responsible for the organization.

"Why are they choosing to come to Genoa?" The question had slipped out of Alessandro's mouth.

---

[2] This is a reference to DELASEM, a delegation with the task of assisting Jewish refugees funded by American charities. The committee was headed by Lelio Vittorio Valobra.

"Ships don't *want* to go to Milan," Lelio said, smiling. It was the last smile of the morning.

There was a flood of refugees, a tidal wave. They were waiting for visas from all over the world: Lisbon, Shanghai, Buenos Aires, Cuba, or Africa. Some of them, perhaps, hoped to stay in Italy. The most prestigious official visas, for Switzerland or the Vatican State, had become a rare privilege.

"Right," Lelio said, as if he were suddenly in a hurry to get away. "In the meantime, we're placing the children in Jewish families here, preferably families with kids." That was how the Rimon family first heard that an eleven-year-old boy called Hermann would be coming to stay with them. But not even Emilia was irritated by the brusque way Lelio had announced the decision.

"Hermann has a sister called Paula," Lelio said, looking pointedly at Alessandro as he leant on the door. "She'll be staying with your aunt."

It was Marc who felt a tiny, but nonetheless irritating, tug of jealousy when he realized that Osvaldo and Wanda had been contacted first.

Emilia couldn't decide. Cesarina's room had been empty for days. Then she made up her mind and pushed the maid's bed into Alessandro's room. She asked her husband, "What do Austrians have for breakfast?" But not even Marc knew.

A woman from the committee who could speak a little German brought Hermann to the house. The boy had dark eyes and brown, curly hair. He clutched his suitcase and stood still in one spot, staring at an armchair upholstered in an ancient cotton flowery print.

"Did you have an armchair like that at home?" Marco asked him in German. The boy managed to nod and then, with a surge of courage, he turned to look at Alessandro. They both followed Marc, who led them to the room where the twin beds had been made up.

The two boys sat on the edge of their beds in silence, like patients waiting for the chief surgeon to come and examine them. When Alessandro was on his own, he would usually lie on his bed with two pillows and read his comic books. Both parents came and stood at the door. Emilia blurted out, "You speak a little Italian, don't you? You must have studied it a little before coming here." Then she slowed down and tried explaining with hand gestures that Alessandro would take him out to see the city.

"I speak little Italian," the boy stammered, looking at Alessandro's comics. He couldn't read the words in the speech bubbles. He went over to Marc and leaned on his arm. Hearing him speak German made him feel grounded. He wanted to go to his sisters, he whispered. Tomorrow, of course. Right now, a little walk, just to get your bearings, Marc said, stroking the boy's hand.

Alessandro walked slowly through the streets he knew so well, as if even his steps needed translating into another language. It felt like he didn't know Italian either. This lazy strolling through streets and piazzas made no sense to him, he was growing tired, so what was Hermann making of it? He turned into the Acquasola Park and walked towards a bench nestled under the overhanging branches of a linden tree. "*Nein*, no!" The boy had stopped in his tracks and looked at him with a terrified expression on his face. "*Juden verboten*," he muttered, pointing at the bench. Alessandro took a second to put two and two together. "We're in Genoa," was all he managed to say. He felt inadequate and stupid. So much for the eleven-year-old who was in the last year of middle school. He had been thinking of taking Hermann skating at the Albaro Lido so that he could meet his friends. Now he thought again.

Jews weren't allowed. Nobody had ever identified them or sent them away, but what if it happened the one time he went along with Hermann?

When he got home, he told his father about the park bench. Marc confirmed that in Vienna Jews were not allowed to sit on benches anywhere, nor could they ride the trams. If anyone tried it, and they were recognized, they would be thrown off with shoves and kicks.

"You don't need to talk about these things with him," Marc said. "He needs a little distraction now, and it's not good for you either." Alessandro couldn't help thinking that he hadn't talked to him about anything. All he had done was walk.

The following morning the two boys went to school together. Hermann was taken straight into the classroom at the back, where the foreign kids of all ages were struggling to learn Italian.

That same day, in the afternoon, Alessandro met Paula for the first time at Aunt Wanda's house. She was really blonde. It was as if the artist had got tired of painting her and had dipped his paintbrush just once to make her light hair an impalpable white cloud. But her steady eyes and strong mouth made her into something more solid. She said "*ciao*" to Alessandro right away in Italian, looking at him with a slightly quizzical smile. Aunt Wanda must have told her they were in the same year at school, but Paula was thirteen and looked every bit like it.

Aunt Wanda knew a lot more about the Berg family. Their father was a famous Viennese watchmaker. He was being put up with his wife by an old couple of Genoese Jews, and they were helping as much as they could with the household chores. Without the help of a maid the couple had been lost.

"On Sunday, you'll meet the whole of the Berg family. I've invited them here for lunch. All of you, too, of course," she added hastily. She had seen that Alessandro's expression had darkened.

CHAPTER 22

Klara Berg was tall and sturdy, her straight blond hair cut at cheek level; the stone from which her daughter had been hewn. Robert and his son Hermann looked as though they had been created with the same formula: they both had disheveled brown hair and dark eyes, though the father's expression was less bewildered than the boy's. The parents looked exhausted; they were determined not to show any other emotion.

Aunt Wanda had taken out the good dinnerware for the occasion and had laid the table beautifully. The lack of a common language disguised their unease. All four members of the Berg family had set out to learn Italian the moment they heard there was a chance they might end up in Italy; they were trying with all the will in the world to throw a phrase or two into the mix, alternating between pride and restraint. Robert and Paula were the most adept at working their way around the labyrinths of the new language, but there were times when Robert Berg had to translate from German with the help of a smattering of French to get to the end of his point.

Emilia asked to sit next to Hermann, opposite his mother Klara, who sat ramrod straight in her chair and limited herself to smiling shyly every now and again. Emilia edged the boy's chair closer, patting him playfully on the arm, and filling his plate with maternal solicitude. Was it her way to reassure Klara? It might have been. For her, teasing and poking her own son was perfectly normal. Alessandro was used to it, though. At home, with no audience at all, she would sit Hermann down and read Alessandro's baby books to him, spelling out each syllable, and then she would rush off and come back with sweets wrapped in shiny paper of different colors that Alessandro had never seen. Hermann tried to refuse, but she insisted, pressing them into his hands fervently. Whenever Nonno Luigi walked past, he would mutter "poor boy" under his breath in Genoese dialect, and it was hard to tell whether he was referring to what had happened to him in Austria occupied by the Germans or to the treatment he was receiving at the hands of his daughter.

After lunch, Klara Berg discreetly drew Hermann into a corner with her and held him close for a long time, whispering every so often in his ear, the boy nodding. When they all withdrew to the sitting room, Osvaldo took over the role of Master of Ceremonies, alternating between French and Italian for no apparent reason. He offered a choice of drinks or liquors, sweets or chocolates, calling out the brand names as if he were an auctioneer. It was all in vain. There was no way a conversation could be had without excluding somebody. Marc was the first to put an end to the charade. He asked Robert in German to talk about his job in Vienna and Robert answered in a whisper.

He had been a clockmaker, Marc translated out loud, and after listening a little longer he felt duty bound to explain: a clockmaker in the widest sense. He had sold and mended all kinds of clocks and watches; at the back of his store there had been a special display case lined with blue velvet where he kept his valuable antique clock collection. As he described his workplace, Robert had suddenly become more animated, outlining the size of the case with his hands in the air, as if he were stroking it.

"Do you see?" Marc said to the family. "He's an artisan and an antiques dealer, all in one. Isn't that's amazing?"

There was no answer. Marc felt his jaw tightening as he looked around the room a little puzzled. Then he realized. What had he been thinking? He had spoken about a place and an occupation that had been violated and destroyed. How could he even think he could talk about these things? His instinct perhaps had been to shed a positive light on their guest, remind everyone that he wasn't born a refugee, but it had been misguided.

The valve that held the wall of water behind the dam had been pulled out, and it was now gushing out. Robert was talking almost to himself in his own language, faster and faster, growing more agitated and emotional.

Marc stopped translating.

Every now and again he launched a furtive glance at his son, his wife, and his in-laws. They were all sitting there grimly, their heads bowed, as if the man's words had mysteriously entered their consciousness by some means other than language. Then he looked over at Robert's wife and children. He felt terrible for them. They understood perfectly. But Hermann, Paula, and their mother were listening intently, completely focused, with a gleam in their eye that could almost be called joy. It was as if Robert had finally unsheathed the sword of justice and was brandishing it in the face of all those people who didn't want to listen, or perhaps didn't believe them, pretending that it was for their own good, that they were helping them to look ahead rather than back.

It was no longer possible to go back to the original spirit of good will with which the Sunday lunch invitation had been made.

As they were saying their goodbyes, before following his family out the door, Alessandro approached Paula. She was staying behind because she had been assigned to live with Aunt Wanda. "I'll come and see you tomorrow," he managed to utter.

It wasn't what he would have liked to say to her, but it was the only thing that came into his mind.

The following day, it was Paula who came to their house with Alessandro's aunt. Wanda had certain errands to run, as Emilia understood immediately when she turned up in a new hat in three shades of gray and a shiny brooch pinned to her coat. "We'll bring the girl home," Emilia said, with a show of mundane politeness, forcing her sister to say when she would he back.

Paula went straight to Alessandro's room, which was now also Hermann's, and stopped at the bookshelves, picking out books and putting them back out of order. She paused when she saw *Vingt mille lieues sous les mers*. "Do you speak French?" she asked in her shaky Italian. "Yes." Alessandro's face lit up. "Do you?"

The girl went quiet, her gaze as evanescent as the ethereal shine of her hair. "No," she said after a moment's pause, shaking her head. "No," she repeated. Then she started chatting to her brother in German. Who knows what she was saying? She even managed to make him laugh.

Later that evening, Emilia asked Alessandro to take the girl back to his aunt's house. She wanted to stay with Hermann and carry on reading the book with colored illustrations. She realized the boy liked it.

Alessandro hoped he wouldn't meet Giamba in the courtyard. His friend knew everything about his love for Alma. He would tease him mercilessly if he saw him with another girl, who was blonde to boot.

They walked without talking most of the way. The sky was gray and the wind was blowing in cruel gusts. His hair blew in wisps in front of his eyes.

"*Ouf, en hiver il fait mauvais même ici,*" Paula mumbled, almost to herself.

"*Mais alors tu parles français. Pourquoi m'as-tu menti?*"

Paula didn't answer at first, then she said softly in French, "My father forbade me to tell you. Your father asked him to."

Alessandro looked at her, baffled. He couldn't understand, or maybe he could no longer understand French, he thought. "Your father doesn't want me to tell you about Vienna; he's worried you'll suffer too much hearing the stories, that it's not good for you. They say it's not good for me, either."

But it was too late. Her French was pouring out, now she had pulled off her gag. Paula would have gone on talking, Alessandro was sure of it. In Hermann's case, it was true that he hadn't studied French, he'd been too young. Best leave him out of these conversations. In his class back home, the teacher had drawn a yellow line across the room and called the Jewish kids out one by one. Their place, she had informed them, was now on the other side of that line. His classmates had red bands with swastikas on them. They had pushed him around and called him names; one of them once had thrown a stone at his forehead. If you looked carefully, you could still see the scar. His parents had stopped sending him to school.

"What about you?"

"I was better off. I was in a private school, but it was pure chance, you know? Pure chance. There are lots of steps down to hell, but it's hell wherever you are. Try and stick that in your brain if you want us to continue to disobey my father and yours."

They had reached the house. Paula ran in. Alessandro had read a lot of novels; the stories were usually about star-crossed lovers with their families against them. Disobeying their fathers was a different matter altogether.

CHAPTER 23

Every day, Emilia waited outside the Jewish school for Hermann to come out early, because his Italian course was only part-time. He wouldn't know how to find his own way home, for sure. His sister Paula and Alessandro—who were in the same class—stayed at least one hour longer. It was hard for Paula to keep up, she was struggling to understand the subjects, but when she did grasp something, there was a flash of light in her eyes as if she had slain the giant Goliath. She took a long time collecting her books, notebooks, and pens and putting on her over-sized coat with its rows of buttons that made it look like a military greatcoat. She would slow down, almost in a trance, as if she were trying to inhabit a space for herself that she hadn't yet created. Then, in tacit agreement, she and Alessandro walked home together. The first time it happened, after chasing a noisy group of friends, Alma stopped and watched them from the sidewalk.

They don't say a word until they turn the corner, then Alessandro stops and enunciates clearly: "*Dis-moi.*" The harsh, imperative tone masks his fear of what he is about to hear. Paula looks compliant and submissive, but she is the one conducting the cruel game. She needs to feed her obsessions, even if it means talking to a boy who's still a kid. This Alessandro looks more mature than her brother, and they have a language in common, which is their shared secret, a mysterious thread that seems to tie them together.

Paula tells her stories quietly, choosing minimal detached

phrases as if she were picking them out one by one and were not allowed to put them together into a unified story.

"1938. Friday, a year ago. Maman is whisking the eggs for the Sabbath fritters. Beating and beating with a fork in a porcelain dish, a lovely sound, like a little march for kids. There are only two days left before the referendum. People vote to decide whether Austria wants to stay a free and independent country. Everyone will vote Yes, it is certain. Another sound. The radio. The Chancellor's voice charged with emotion. He's saying there will no longer be a referendum, that he has been asked personally to hand in his resignation. He'll do it. Otherwise the German troops, already deployed at the borders, will occupy the country. We're silent, completely still. I look at my father; maybe he will tell me it is all a joke, but I know that is not the case. Maman stares at a dot on the window; a street light has just gone on.

"The whisked eggs abandoned in the plate are slowly sinking. The Chancellor says he's accepted this terrible imposition to avert a bloodbath.

"'God Save Austria!' he shouts, sobbing. An old man sobbing on the radio. Mamma and Papà are also crying. We are all crying. They play the national anthem for the last time on the radio. Then, to fill in the silence, timidly, almost afraid, the notes of Beethoven's First Symphony.

"Outside, the roar of a raging storm, people shouting '*Heil Hitler*!', '*Sieg Heil*!' And even louder, '*Juden verreck*!', Die Jews! Still louder, outside, the deafening sound of taxis, buses and private cars going crazy sounding their horns. The insistent ringing of the tram sounds like the death knell: *Remember you will die.*

"We look out of the window, shielding ourselves with the curtains.

"Thousands and thousands of people are out there in black

shirts and red armbands with swastikas on them. Where were they hiding those uniforms that they could get them out so quickly? The buses, trams, and cleaning trucks have the same horrible symbol painted on their sides. People laughing and waving flags are thronging into the streets.

"By 11 P.M. it's official. The Nazi flag has been hung like laundry on every important building in the city.

"Later the radio announces we have a new Chancellor. 'Austria is finally National-Socialist,' they shout in celebration. We're still there behind the curtains. Maybe we feel the mauve damask curtains my mother sewed by hand for eighteen consecutive months will protect us forever. The *others* are already inside my father's store. They are throwing stones from a distance, just for fun, and shattering the glass with bats and rifle butts. They wreck everything: the shelves, the lamps, the clocks. There is no trace of the Russian gold-and-blue-enamel clock anywhere, even among the smithereens on the floor. Papa realizes as soon as he walks in the next morning at dawn. The only thing left is a big black *J* painted on the last hanging piece of the store window.

"A few days later the store is confiscated. Papa has to go on paying taxes for the property he no longer owns."

They reached Aunt Wanda's front door. Paula came to an abrupt halt and stopped talking. Alessandro urged her to go on, he wanted to know more, but it was as if the girl had run out of stories. She was stuck on this one. She wanted him to realize how the world can change in the space of a rest between notes. In the slice of time between Beethoven and the swastikas there was her: Paula Berg, who was thirteen that March 11, and at midnight, at the dawn of March 12, she would turn fourteen. At thirteen, she was a young Austrian citizen, at fourteen she was a beetle to be crushed underfoot, with Beethoven playing in the background.

"Vienna changed overnight into a Vienna that no longer exists." Her voice had become dreamy and distant.

Alessandro recognized the classical reference, and it bothered him. Showing off in this situation felt sacrilegious, and completely off. He had gotten to know the family, and he felt an urge to participate in their history. That was all. But it also felt as though the girl's feet, words, and thoughts were still glued to a central point in her life that was called Vienna. The Nazis yelling and wrecking property were all Austrians. The Germans had moved in later. They were all Austrians; even Frau Elfriede was Austrian.

"Who's Frau Elfriede?" Alessandro murmured, disconcerted.

"No, that's enough. Your aunt and uncle are waiting for me for lunch." She had stopped speaking French, acting as if she didn't even understand it. "Other time. We speak other time," she said in her broken Italian.

Aunt Wanda had spotted her from the window. They had been standing by the front door for a while. She thought they were in love, as did her sister. "I thought he liked that other girl at school," Emilia grumbled.

Marc wasn't convinced. He kept an eye on his son, but all he saw was anguish, not love.

The following day at school, Alma asked him, "What language do you and the Austrian girl speak to one another in?"

"Italian, of course," Alessandro answered hastily.

"Really?" Alma smiled, walking ahead and turning around to repeat, "Really?"

Chapter 24

F rau Elfriede Tipper was the neighbor who had lived in the apartment below them. She had two kids—a boy and a girl—just like them, but they were no longer children, and Elfriede always gave the young kids upstairs sweets and let them win at cards or bingo. They would thank her with a bow.

Elfriede would always say, stroking Hermann's head, "How lovely it must be to still have little ones at home."

After the night of murderous yelling, bludgeoning, and waving of swastikas, most of their neighbors turned away when they crossed paths with anyone in the Berg family. Some muttered threats under their breath. Others just speeded up their pace and looked down. Frau Elfriede was the only one who said hello to them, as she always had. Her attitude was *complaisant*, Paula explained, as though she was looking down on them.

Her father said it was stupid to say that, but he understood. His children had become over-sensitive.

One day Elfriede stopped Mrs. Berg on the landing to announce with a huge smile on her face that she had great news: her daughter was getting married. Klara said congratulations, she was happy for her, best wishes, and a few other appropriate words. Back home, she used to sometimes shake her head and say, "If only that Tipper girl had one physical defect, at least I'd remember something about her. I forget what she looks like. Literally none of her features stick with me." Now there was someone who not only recognized her but wanted to marry her.

She asked Frau Tipper anxiously, "Will the newlyweds be staying in town? Will they stay close?"

"Yes, very close," Elfriede smiled, wagging her finger jokingly.

"Right there." She pointed her finger up at the floor above.

"There?" Klara asked.

"Yes." Frau Tipper bowed her head almost solemnly.

Then she went straight into practical matters. "The eviction decree is ready, but we don't need to go that far, do we? We can wait another week and come to an agreement, I'm sure, as to which pieces of furniture we'd like to keep. We'll pay, of course."

They left at the end of the seventh day, each carrying a suitcase. Hermann had filled his with books and colored pencils, and his mother had said nothing. A few essential items and two boxes had already been taken away on a cart pulled by a limping, half-blind horse.

In a cloth bag, Klara carried the three jars of homemade jam Frau Tippler had given her in lieu of payment for the things they'd left behind.

A much older cousin of their father's took them into her bare lodgings. Her husband, Peter, had been arrested, and Irma spent most of her days wandering around looking for news of him. No one knew where they took people who were arrested; they could have been taken anywhere before being transported to Dachau.

Peter returned three days later.

Not even his wife recognized him.

He'd been kept three days in a cellar, hadn't been allowed to wash or shave, and his belt and shoes had been removed.

He knocked on the door and stood there, barefoot, bent double holding up his pants, with a disheveled beard. He was the caricature of a degenerate Jew wandering around the streets of Vienna—straight out of a cartoon strip from *Stürmer*. That was what they wanted. Peter Roth was a lawyer in a big, private firm. The Gestapo had freed him once he'd signed a form handing over his property to the state. They had already confiscated the family home.

Irma looked at her husband, dumbstruck. It would have felt sacrilegious to cry or comfort him in any way. Tragedies like this should be respected. She dropped into a chair as if she were performing *shivah* and didn't move again.

Hermann shut himself in the bedroom and didn't want to come out.

Where could he go, anyway? Jews were not allowed to wear the swastika armband, but if you weren't wearing one, they would grab you and rough you up. Paula and Hermann were scared of going to the park and seeing those benches "reserved for Aryans." They had to be constantly wary whenever they were out and about. If a group of people waving flags approached, you had to run and hide in a doorway. If you didn't raise your arm in a Nazi salute, you were beaten up by the crowd, but a Jew couldn't . . .

Paula had stopped talking one day. They were walking their usual way and she stopped every now and again to look at store windows, the pharmacy, or a lady's hat trimmed with a mass of ribbons.

"You're not done yet . . ." Alessandro murmured.

"Am I supposed to tell you the whole story in chapters? Kristallnacht, what we heard about relatives and friends arrested on the street? Or do you want to know about the lines my father had to stand in, day after day, in front of the embassy of this or that country to try and get a visa? The answer was always the same: 'Our quotas have already been filled.' And he had to go back home."

"You're here now," Alessandro said, confused.

"Italy has been everything for us. They got us away just before we were thrown into the fire. We'll never forget it, of course. I have nothing else to say to you." She started striding ahead of him, forcing Alessandro to break into a run to keep up with her.

"That's enough now!" Paula had stopped in her tracks, as if she were challenging an unwelcome suitor. "I told you some of my stuff because I thought you needed to know, but at some point, we need to stop. Only old people want to talk about the past all the time," she said. Then she added, to Alessandro's surprise, "I've had enough of speaking French, too. Why should we put both our fathers' backs up?" Finally, she murmured almost to herself, "At times like these we need our fathers to protect us."

After her tirade, she went straight back to normal, as evanescent as the color of her hair. Her Italian had come along remarkably; she wanted to learn the language perfectly. She asked him about Alma. "We're just friends," Alessandro mumbled. He didn't like the new tone Paula had adopted. It felt inappropriate and somehow disrespectful of what had passed between them, and what they had shared—if briefly. She was putting a dent in *his own* suffering but she went on regardless. Was he in love with Alma? In love? That was a joke, he was a twelve-year-old schoolboy and she was fourteen! It was . . . a deep friendship. Well, that was what Alma called it. Paula giggled absentmindedly.

The two girls started spending all their time together. Alessandro couldn't swear to it, but he was pretty sure they were speaking French. Of course, Alma didn't have a father telling her not to.

The family set sail under the June sun in 1939. They had arrived at the beginning of the year, when the wind was still icy. War was brewing in Europe, and the association had been frantically scrabbling to get as many visas as possible for the refugees who had been temporarily accommodated in Genoa. After a long and delicate process, secretly guided from the shadows, the Bergs were finally issued a visa: destination, Singapore.

The two families that had hosted them were not allowed to wave them off from the docks; their departure was to take place at dawn, with the utmost discretion. For their farewells, they met on the last Sunday at the Rimon home. As soon as Hermann saw his mother, he grabbed her arm and wouldn't let go.

Two days later, Emilia asked her son to give her a hand. "We need to take the bed back to Cesarina's room."

Then she said to her husband, "The British Consulate called. They say to call back."

CHAPTER 25

He slumped down in the armchair; his inert limbs and his eyes darting around in anguish spoke two entirely different languages. Emilia didn't appreciate either one of them. Alessandro waited.

"What did the Embassy want?" Emilia asked, making an effort to sound disinterested.

"It was the Consulate," Marc snapped, in order to buy a little time. "They think we're in danger and have offered to help. That is, they have a specific plan for us," he said looking Emilia straight in the eye. Emilia was already on the defensive. Where was this entirely new danger coming from? Who asked the Embassy to help us, anyway?

"Do you really think Hitler has changed?" Europe had lain prostrate at his feet the year before and was now handing over half of Czechoslovakia. In exchange for peace, anything is possible, it was proclaimed. Europe rejoiced. "Hitler didn't stop, though, did he? He took Bohemia and Moravia, and now he wants Poland. They won't let him have Poland; there will be war." Marc tried to throw as many facts as he could at her.

"That's what you've been saying to Osvaldo and my sister, who's always got her nose in everywhere," Emilia said defiantly, folding the tablecloths and matching napkins and attempting to iron them out with the palms of her hands. "I just don't get why the Embassy suddenly feels the need to discuss politics with you," she muttered.

"I just told you, the Consulate has made a specific plan for us," Marc said, pronouncing every syllable slowly and clearly. His gaze wandered out the window, as if he could already see on the horizon a world that adopted a different alphabet: a war, Italy siding with Hitler, he and his family becoming enemy aliens, arrest, prison. Marc spoke in a neutral tone of voice, almost calmly. He now knew there was a solution out there waiting for them at the end of the road. "The Consulate will take care of all the details of our move to England. Money, valuables, and my work tools will be sent by diplomatic pouch." This was the news that he had wanted to impart at the beginning of the conversation. "They're saving us," he said almost in a whisper, discomfited.

There was a long silence. Emilia's heavy palms hitting the tablecloth sounded like punches in a boxing ring.

"Italy will never join the war. If other countries want to do so, they're welcome; it's their own business." She looked up at her husband. "And you? Are you really ready to say, 'Yes, thanks, I'll move to England,' just like that? Who do you know there? His Majesty, the King?" Vaguely sorry for her outburst, she added, "There aren't any dangers here. We've always done well. You're working as much as before, our boy's Jewish school is better than the other schools. What about the Austrians? Who took them in when nobody else wanted them? We Italians did. We're not bad people in the end. Granted, there are restrictions in place for Jews, but it's got to be better than becoming refugees ourselves."

"It's not true that we're doing well here. I feel humiliated. Always. I don't want to end up like Hermann." Alessandro's voice resounded like an unexpected noise in the night. They had forgotten he was even there.

"Hermann! I knew it. I could see that you were always jealous of that poor little boy whenever I tried to console him." Emilia had stopped wrestling with the tablecloths and had sat down with her hands in her lap. Marc stopped his wife's clumsy attempt to change the subject in its tracks.

"We've talked and talked about whether to leave or whether to stay. Before it was all in theory, but now it's different. We have a concrete proposal. That makes all the difference. Can't you see?"

Emilia went on trying to wriggle out of the conversation; she wouldn't let herself be dragged into it. If he was such an attentive parent, did he know that his son had disobeyed him and spoken French to that presumptuous little Austrian girl? She'd told him all sorts of terrible things, but they'd all taken place in other countries. It was quite right that Germans and Austrians were running. But Italians didn't need to. You don't leave your home and family behind just because you've talked to some Consul with a bee in his bonnet.

Marc put his arm on the table and with a tired gesture swept away all the silverware his wife had been laying out. All her predictable objections served no other purpose than to keep the real problems out of the picture. He started again, in the same meticulous way he worked on his gems, patiently going over all the salient points: the war, being foreign nationals, the advantages of holding an alternative passport . . . Emilia rolled her eyes just as she did when her father started going on about his experience as a railway man. "I'm not leaving. I will not leave Italy to go who knows where."

"Mamma!" Alessandro had thrown himself on her, holding her convulsively. "You're only thinking about yourself. As if I don't exist. Aren't mothers supposed to save their own children before they save themselves? Let's go before it's too late."

Emilia gazed at him, shaking her head. "Yes, you're my son, but what do you know about these things? Do you think you're so intelligent that you can predict what's going to happen in Italy in the future? Who put these ideas into your head?"

Alessandro had already run into his room by the time Marc

murmured, "You can say that about our son . . . but what about me? Do you think I'm not able to reason?"

"You're good at your job, but you are completely impractical," Emilia huffed, picking up the last tablecloths that needed folding.

On September 1, 1939, the German army marched into Poland. France and Great Britain reacted immediately, declaring war. Italy stayed out at the beginning. Not that it was neutral: Mussolini didn't like the word; it was too bourgeois. He preferred to call it "non-belligerence."

Alessandro is on a train. It's still the school vacation, and he and Aunt Wanda are visiting a cousin who won the Lotto and built a little villa in Voghera with the proceeds. The family had talked about the win a great deal because the numbers he used had been dictated in his dreams by a deceased grandfather.

Three women in their compartment are talking about the *Blitzkrieg*, filled with admiration for Hitler's astuteness and agility in conducting his lightning strikes. Alessandro joins in the conversation as if it were completely normal: a simple exchange of opinions. He explains his views on Hitler, Germany, Nazism in an animated tone, his guard down.

The slap lands square on his cheek while he is going full steam. He sways. Not because of the slap. His whole being, heart and mind finally allied, is ready and aching to strike back, but the cage of his twelve-year-old body prevents movement. He would look ridiculous, like a kitten that could be picked up by the collar with one finger and hurled into the distance. Wanda, wearing her beautiful necklace and crisscross leather shoes, is paralyzed. There is nobody to complain to if the person who has been struck is a Jew. They would be putting themselves in even greater danger. She mumbles a few bland and deliberately incomprehensible words of protest, grabs her nephew by the hand, and drags him to another compartment. In their new seats, his aunt drops her head like a little bird and prepares to go to sleep.

Slumped there with his head down, Alessandro mutters, "I want to leave." His aunt reassures him that they'll only be staying at the villa for a couple of days and that they're sure to have a lovely time.

CHAPTER 26

Alma says, "You've changed your timetable." Alessandro doesn't get it. "When your Austrian friend was here, you had your private lessons in the afternoon; now, you've gone back to doing them straight after school."

What was the point of Alma's punctilious study of his schedule, as if he were running a railway? Alma explains the point right away, "You shifted all your lessons around because you wanted to walk home with her." Alessandro simply nods. He will not give Alma the satisfaction.

Alessandro started after-school Hebrew lessons with a teacher the rabbi had recommended almost a year ago. The times of their sessions have changed continually, and now that his bar mitzvah is approaching, he has more lessons scheduled. Walking with his Austrian friend is a thing of the past; now he has extra lessons in the afternoon to attend. He can't afford to stop practicing. It isn't just a matter of reading that day's portion of the *parashah* in Hebrew; he also has to chant it, following the most complete form of the rite.

He's more worried about performing in public in a packed synagogue than about taking the exam with Rabbi Bonfiglioli in a few days.

The rabbi receives him in the same dark-furniture office his mother dragged him to years ago. The inkwell in the shape of a globe held up by four muscular figures is still there on his desk. He looks at it exactly as he did then.

"The moment you get to study the Torah has finally come!" The rabbi seems to remember what he said to eight-year-old Alessandro. He's seen him hundreds of times at the Jewish school, but they've never talked about private things. They talked about everything else, even the parties the children held.

The rabbi asks him to sit down on the other side of his desk. "Tell me," he murmurs, with a sad smile. Tell him what? He's the examiner; he's supposed to ask me things. The rabbi knows the boy has been coached in religious strictures, prayers, blessings, festivities, Jewish history. He's confident the boy is well prepared. "Tell me what you have personally learned from the *Terumah*, the *parashah* you will be reading next Saturday."

"*Terumah* means 'gift' or 'offering' but also 'elevation.'" Alessandro starts talking and doesn't stop; then he realizes he's behaving as if he were doing a test at school, saying as much as possible to prove he's mugged up on everything. This is not what he wanted. Actually, he dreamed of the exact opposite: an exchange of distilled wisdom. But he couldn't help it; he'd been taken by a form of childish regression. He needed to show he knew his stuff. "*Terumah* is literally a gift, an offering to build a portable tabernacle, a sanctuary in the desert. Gold and precious stones were also offered, but, as I was saying, the true meaning is elevation."

The rabbi doesn't say a word. He isn't frowning, but he doesn't look happy either. Alessandro is getting anxious. He wants to make things right, explain the concept better, use his own words. He tries again. "The offer is elevation because you have to give something up to give it to someone else. If you succeed in elevating yourself by giving to others, then the whole world can be elevated. In short, giving elevates the world. I think this is the significance of the text, or at least that's what my teacher has helped me understand. That's how I see it, though I may be wrong."

Rabbi Bonfiglioli still says nothing, but now he's smiling.

"Rabbi, you're not saying anything," Alessandro blurts out, fidgeting on his chair.

"Silence is a fence for wisdom," the rabbi recites. "Don't you know the *Mishnah*? You need to learn this section." Then he murmurs, "You'll go on studying and become a good Jew."

Alessandro is embarrassed. He's enjoying the moment, but he's not at all sure he'll be a good Jew.

They start talking about everyday things such as which relatives are coming from other cities and how packed the synagogue will be. Everybody knows two parties have been planned: one with adults and one just for kids. "You've turned thirteen now; you'll be allowed to dance," the rabbi teased. A younger boy will be winding up the gramophone this time. Your family was good to take in the Austrian children; you know they've arrived safely in Singapore, don't you? What about school? The rabbi sighs. Alessandro's report cards hadn't changed; he had top marks in some subjects, and average grades in others.

Alessandro thinks that the rabbi can speak easily about ordinary, everyday life. Who knows? He may even be a fan of the Genoa soccer team.

He is just getting up and preparing to leave when Rabbi Bonfiglioli calls him back with a gesture. "I know you're not deeply religious, and maybe you never will be, but I can see you feel the tradition. Tradition is a tree. If a leaf is not attached to a tree it dries up and drops off, and in no time at all it is no longer even a leaf."

His relatives were all there in the crowded synagogue; it was like a repeat of the meeting two years ago at the seafront villa in Ardenza, near Livorno, only a little smaller. The matriarch Edith was missing. Everyone knew she was quietly fading away in her bed, bidding farewell to life as elegantly as she had lived it. The others were there as proof that they were not only still

alive, but also ready to celebrate every joyful Jewish ritual
afforded them with singing, dancing, and praying.

Sitting in the front row next to his father, Alessandro waited
to be called up to the altar. Nerves gave sudden, violent lurches
in his belly. Apart from that, he felt empty; surrounded by religious men whose face he was unable to distinguish, he felt
utterly alone. Maybe the synagogue and its devotees didn't
really exist. Could the whole place be a projection of his own
vague, capricious search for meaning? He didn't believe in
them, and there was no reason why they should believe in him.
He was deceiving them.

He found himself up on the *tevah*. His musical ear was perhaps short of being perfect, but nonetheless his chanting rose
into the air, mysteriously gathering strength. The world around
him suddenly came into focus; he recognized his Jewish brothers
one by one. The older women in their best clothes behind the
grate, clutching their *tefillin*, were dots of color in a painting,
and among the men he was able to pick out the believers, the
lost souls, the ones who had dragged themselves there, those
who could see the apocalypse coming, and those for whom hope
sprung eternal—they were all cloaked by a heavy pall of fore-
boding weighing down on their heads. Only once he had
stopped singing, after the rabbi and all the others had hugged
and congratulated him, did this thought come into his mind.

They've taken everything away from us, but if there is something—call it what you will—that they have given us, we
should try and proclaim it, even if it is just rhetoric. They have
given us, by means of force, an identity. Many of us didn't ask
for it, others had no intention of owning it, but that is how
things have ended up. Now that they have thrown us this lifeline, it would be foolish not to grab hold of it. Without the
rope, we would be even more of a nothing than we already are.

Aunt Wanda hosted the reception for the extended family.

The endless shouting of *lechaim*, together with bizarre improvised speeches, went on for hours. The guests were reclining on the sofas or settled into the armchairs; they were clearly in no hurry to catch their trains or take the tram home.

Alessandro walked home, his parents trotting behind him. The real party was to be held at his house. Two friends had gotten the time wrong and were already waiting for him at the front door.

They had put the extra boards in to extend the table and thrown a white tablecloth over it, with a smaller, light blue cloth on top; this was their only timid attempt at invoking a Jewish symbol. The sandwiches, cookies, buns, and jugs of orangeade, fizzy lemonade, and cherry syrup, with a few real cherries thrown in, slightly ruined the effect, however. The focal point of the room was the gramophone, which occupied almost the whole of the end wall. A pale, mangy little cousin called Guido was given the task of winding the handle. The boy smiled shyly when he looked up, but once he took on the role in earnest, he proved invaluable, becoming almost authoritarian.

Alma was there. She was wearing a green suit with a copper shine, with a little cream handbag borrowed from her mother slung over her shoulder. She looked beautiful. Just looking at her made Alessandro tremendously happy and tremendously sad at the same time. He had decided not to ask her for the first dance. Was their friendship a deep one, as Alma had once claimed? Maybe it was. Alma didn't treat him like a little brother that needed indulging; they talked for hours and they could confront one another. But it wasn't enough for him. He'd just turned thirteen, and she was over fifteen. When would their respective ages become so irrelevant that it would no longer be an issue between them? In seven years? Or would seven years still not be sufficient, requiring seven more, like the patriarch Job with Rachel?

Alessandro chose Rita as his first dancing partner. She was fourteen, with braids, a rosy complexion, and the firm body of a Russian athlete. Alma smiled in the same way she had done the day she'd seen him walk away after school with Paula, the Austrian girl.

The needle glided smoothly over the record, and the couples danced the tango listening to hits like "Maria de la O," or "Caminito."

When the young crowd, at the suggestion of some of the fathers, started shouting one *mazel tov* after another, Alessandro found his arms linked with the only person he really cared about at the party.

That evening, they were tidying up the living room and the kitchen, trying to keep Nonno Luigi away, who had gathered all the wrapped presents he had collected together in a laundry basket and was picking them out, guessing who had given what, and roughly how much each person had spent. Alessandro turned to him and murmured, "Later, Nonno."

It was quiet again. There was just one relative staying the night who had to catch a train back to Milan early in the morning.

Emilia dropped into an armchair, exhausted. She looked at her son. "You have no excuses now. Next Saturday you'll come to synagogue with me, won't you?"

"You don't get it do you?" Alessandro yelled. Then, in a quiet, dejected tone, he mumbled to himself, "Nobody gets it, nobody gets anything."

Precisely one week after the party, two policemen came to the door. They had come to confiscate Marc's license. Members of the Jewish race were not allowed to be craftsmen.

There was no need to call Osvaldo. He called them himself to say that his license had been taken away that day, too. He was no longer allowed to own a store.

CHAPTER 27

S o, they took away your license, but what does that change?"

Emilia took her husband's grim refusal to move on as a personal affront. "For Osvaldo, I get it. He's had a few problems. He's had to sign the store over to someone else, but things are going well for him. He's chosen someone he can really, really trust." Trying to catch Marc's eye, she went on muttering, "That's the way to go about things. Getting depressed is a waste of time."

Her husband didn't answer, and Emilia was stunned. He'd always managed to produce some sort of rebuttal; he was far too polite just to sit there in silence. Two years before, she continued, when the Laws came out, they'd been worried about losing his license, and then it hadn't even been taken away. They already knew back then that, even if he did lose his license, he'd never lose his clients. "They come to you because they value you, not for a piece of paper they hardly know exists."

"I don't feel well," Marc murmured, rubbing his belly as if he were trying to soothe a pain caused by a punch someone had given him right there in the stomach.

"You must have eaten too much at the bar mitzvah. It was non-stop eating: lunch, the afternoon party, and then dinner." Emilia looked sideways at her husband and felt the first grumblings of doubt. Marc confessed he had a little fever, and Emilia immediately called Dr. Marcenaro. While the doctor was examining him, Marc leaped up, mumbling "My mother, my mother," his speech slurred, and promptly collapsed to the ground.

"When you're about to die, it's more normal to shout 'Mamma' than 'My mother!'" Emilia tried to joke. She hadn't left the chair by her husband's hospital bedside in days and, for the first time, saw he was feeling a little better. A heart attack while a doctor was right there on hand examining you was more than a stroke of luck: it was a good omen. Emilia was very pleased with herself for having had the inspiration to call the old family doctor that morning.

It was the first time they'd allowed Alessandro to come to the hospital, and the boy stared at his father with the same horrified expression he had had when he saw his being taken away in an ambulance as he came home from school for lunch.

"My mother . . ." Marc smiled at his son. "I wasn't summoning her! I was just trying to say that nobody would ever have taken my mother's license away."

"So?" Emilia jumped out of her seat. "Are you proposing we all move to Holland?"

"Don't be stupid," Marc sighed. It was just a thought, like the hundreds of others that had crowded his mind recently. He didn't want to talk about it. He turned to his son and started asking about school.

He was discharged a month later and sent home with a long list of recommendations, strict doctors' orders, and boxes of medicine. He went straight back to work, where clients awaited him and congratulated him on his return to good health. One couple had even gone to visit him in hospital. Emilia took to visiting Marc in his workshop at regular intervals and, with an immutable expression of perennial disapproval, she handed him the brown pill and the white one, with a glass of water on a saucer.

It was now spring, and the air was filled with enticements. There seemed to be little or no fighting going on at the front. The war was like a cat snoozing by the fire. Hitler had taken Czechoslovakia and Poland, and then Denmark and Norway, but the final assault on the heartland of France felt like it was hanging in the air. The two sides kept their distance and watched out for when the other would make the first move, which never seemed to happen.

Alessandro felt a perhaps unjustified, but nonetheless comfortable, sense of calm growing inside him. His father was almost completely recovered and was working as hard as ever; school and everything else was the same as usual. Alma felt like a friend again. The same image that had come to his mind before returned to haunt him: the derailed train continuing its course over devastated terrain, the impervious craters ever deepening.

The German invasion of the low countries began on the morning of May 10, 1940. As airports and bridges were carpet bombed, the paratroopers had already been dropped from the sky to occupy every inch of the enemy territory. Belgium and the Netherlands were obliterated in a flash. Four days later, with Rotterdam razed to the ground, Holland was on its knees and ready to surrender. The Allies, desperately called to come to their aid, were powerless. British and French commanders had been tricked, and now they were the ones attempting in vain to head off German troops as they advanced across France to the coast. Only ten days had gone by, and British troops were being evacuated *en masse* from the beaches of Dunkirk, with a fleet of motor vessels and private boats. The French went on defending their country, but they had been abandoned and hounded, and had lost faith and energy.

"And there you were, so keen to move to Holland!" Emilia

preened. She was as shocked as Marc, but she couldn't resist her usual baiting.

"I *never*, not even *once*, expressed any intention whatsoever of moving to Holland." Marc spoke to his unsuspecting brother-in-law in an irate tone, because he didn't want to talk to his wife.

Hitler's surprise thrust into Western Europe had been a success. They were all devastated by the news and, in their bewilderment, had started calling family gatherings at short notice. They got together to talk, but then they sat in silence for hours. What was there to discuss?

"Do you have any news of your mother?" Wanda asked Marc.

Marc sighed. "She has some dear friends who live in the countryside. I hope she's gone to stay with them."

"I'm sure she has," Wanda was quick to respond. She was happy to have broken the ice, at least. "If things go on like this, the war may be over in a few days," she ventured. She managed to sound concerned, but somewhere inside her there was the guilty seed of hope that she could never confess. Once everything was over, however bad it was, at least it was over.

"What are you talking about?" Osvaldo was livid. "The war may be *over*? The right word for where we are now is a *cliff-edge*, one we'll all be disappearing over."

"Great Britain is tenacious. It won't capitulate easily," Marc murmured.

What could they know? He and his brother-in-law were nothing more than two ordinary people, gripping onto whatever hope there was when even the sea was licked with flames.

At the movies. Alessandro with Alma and Marina, a sharp young girl with dark, intelligent eyes. They'd dragged him to see *Le Paradis Perdu*, a romantic film about star-crossed lovers with the war as a backdrop, and if he were honest, he was happy to be there. In the stalls, the women at the matinee show gasped and commented, or called out to their friends who came in late in strangled voices. Alessandro had always found them irritating, but this time it was really too much. They were shouting; one of them got up from the back row and was carrying on as if she were in the middle of the road, waving her arms around. When the lights went on and they left the theater, there were crowds pushing and shoving. People were running, and their voices blended with one voice that was louder than all the others, blasting from all sides, including the tops of the trees.

The apocalyptic words Mussolini was declaiming over the loudspeakers echoed all over. The *Duce* was broadcasting his message to the world: "A declaration of war has already been handed to the Ambassadors of Great Britain and France. There is only one order: conquer! And we will conquer! Italian people, rush to arms . . ." His words, before a jubilant crowd, were the final seal.

It was June 10, 1940, a beautiful summer's day.

Alessandro almost flew home. His father looked up, a dead expression on his face; his mother was cooking and didn't lift her eyes from the stove.

The following day, the British RAF started bombing Genoa, and the French followed suit two days later. But the Rimon family, by that point, was already behind bars at the central police station.

CHAPTER 28

"C itizen of an enemy country" the policeman announced, squinting at the sheet that was dangling from his left hand as if it were a duster. He was short and stocky, with the big gnarled hands of a peasant's son. Standing by his side, a skinny young man gave them a long, bovine stare.

It had taken a while for Marc to ascertain that they were actually under arrest, partly because the officer was hesitant and unable to articulate, grunting intermittently. Perhaps even he hadn't quite grasped who on earth these people, who were answering his questions calmly in his own language, were.

"Bring some things with you." The policeman moved on to more familiar territory, his tone growing more confident accordingly. "You will not be coming back home this evening."

"Not even the child?" Emilia had burst out.

"What child? If he were one of ours, he would have signed up already," the skinny officer had quipped, attempting in vain to make his partner smirk.

They each moved around the house attending to their own things. Emilia shouted to Alessandro in the next-door room to grab a sweater, even though it was June and already quite warm.

They had already gathered in the hall when, from the end of the corridor, Nonno Luigi appeared, pale in the face but straight as a ramrod.

"Who are you?" the officer had asked, staring at the sheet. His name was not on it.

"He's my father," Emilia sighed.

"Are you foreign, too?"

"I'm Italian," Luigi answered, his voice vibrant with indignation. How could he be anything but Italian when he'd worked all his life as a trusted employee of the state railways? The policeman had interpreted his tone as one of national pride. "Hail Comrade!" he had said, raising his arm in a Fascist salute.

There was no way on earth that Emilia would ever ask her husband and son for forgiveness, not even with a quick glance in their direction. Marc and Alessandro, for their part, would never allow the words of accusation that seemed to hum in the air of the dirty gray cell to escape their lips.

At one point, Emilia said, "It's all a mistake," but neither of them answered.

An extremely early dinner had been brought to their cell, and the family understood that the three camp beds placed against the walls would be their resting place that night.

When Alessandro extracted a pair of pajamas from his bag, Emilia tried to contain her anger but failed.

"Pajamas! How on earth could you think of packing pajamas as if you were a little lord going on vacation when we're staying in a hell hole like this? Which we'll be leaving any time now," she added hesitantly.

Alessandro gave her a sullen stare in return.

"He packed on his own; maybe we should have helped him," Marc said although he didn't feel at all guilty. He had left him to his own devices deliberately to give him a sense that he was his own master at such a traumatic moment.

"It wasn't a mistake. I chose them on purpose." Alessandro rummaged in his bag and triumphantly produced the gold chain with the Star of David pendant his grandmother had left him. "I didn't know where to hide it, and I thought nobody would look in a pajama pocket." He had also secured it with a safety pin so that it wouldn't drop out.

Emilia turned her head away from him, looking at the wall. "You see? Do you realize now how stupid and childish your son is?" she yelled at her husband. Nonno Luigi would obviously have taken the chain out of the drawer and given it to Wanda to take care of, but the kid had to come up with some brilliant idea, and he carries on pretending he's a genius when he's not.

"We all make mistakes," Marc answered dryly, and Emilia suddenly went quiet.

In the dark that fell early in the cell, even the distant chime from the church tower ringing hour after hour was tinged with evil. Alessandro was overtaken by anguish, which stifled him. It wasn't the situation that caused it—in fact, a part of him was curious—but his mother, as usual.

If they had at least waged open war over the years and railed against one another to defend opposing views, even if she had won a few of them, it wouldn't have been so bad. The battles would have strengthened him as he grew up. But this had not been the case.

His mother sewed his buttons back on his shirts, brushed his clothes down, insisted he ate fruit after lunch and dinner, and shouted at random intervals into the other room urging him to study harder. But the truth was something else. Spinning a sticky web around her son and capturing him in the silk threads of her contempt was the way Emilia Rimon, née Dello Strologo, waged her open war. Her scorn took Alessandro's fight away and made him insecure. It was easier for him to conquer her reluctant love than to break out of the elusive web that made him a laughing-stock every time he said or did anything. In the world outside, he could be brilliant and funny, and people liked him for it, but this only irritated his mother more. Increasingly, he found himself doing things that made no sense, or saying things that sounded absurd, in her presence. Putting the gold chain in his pajama pocket had been a stupid thing to do. Maybe.

"There's a relative of yours here. I'll give you five minutes, no more. The chief's not in today; he's seeing his son off to war." The officer had said this almost apologetically, as if he needed a justification. He wasn't sure whether prisoners were allowed to have visitors. The well-dressed gentleman hadn't said he was a lawyer, either. He'd been pretty insistent, for sure, and he behaved and spoke like a figure of authority. The policeman had ended up giving his consent without even realizing he'd done it. In any case, the prisoner accompanied by his wife and son didn't look too dangerous.

"Osvaldo!" A few steps away from the grate that had just been opened for him, Marc felt he had regained a long-awaited freedom even though only a few hours had gone by since they'd been picked up.

"Listen, Osvaldo," he started, convulsively. "You must go and speak to the people at the Consulate to see if they can still help me."

His brother-in-law was stunned. He liked to think of himself as being the one who was always well-informed, with privileged sources, but it was usually Marc who came out as the leading force in their discussions. Marc was the one who knew things, thought about them, and came up with the ideas. If he was lost, then they were all in trouble.

"What are you talking about? The Consulate had to close on the double. The Rome Embassy warned them just in time. They shredded all the documents and made it back home before it was too late."

"Of course." Marc looked down. "I'm so stupid!" For a moment, Osvaldo was almost relieved.

They carried on talking hastily. The chief would be back the following day, and Osvaldo had already contacted someone who might be able to help them untangle his case. After all, Marc had a wife and son who were both Italian. But . . .

"Three days ago, you bombed us here in Genoa." Osvaldo tried to turn it into a joke to lighten up the atmosphere, but Marc's face was grim. Even the family saw him as an alien; worse, as an enemy alien.

"Tomorrow he'll come and talk to the chief," Marc summarized hurriedly when he got back into the cell. Alessandro saw how deeply humiliated his father was and felt sad for him. He took his pajama top and, looking straight at his mother, put it on over his shirt.

There wasn't even the comfort of dark in the tiny room; the yellowish glow of a lightbulb was there to remind you of what you were. Alessandro tried to think of Alma. He tried to convince himself that he was happy because her family was Italian, and so there was no way she would end up in a prison cell like them. It was just artificial reasoning produced by his brain; there was no feeling behind it.

CHAPTER 29

H e behaved more like the proprietor of a miserable boarding house than a member of the police force. The officer they had gotten to know well arrived early that morning carrying a tray with a cup of barley coffee and a slice of bread each.

"Are you English?" the gnarled-handed policeman asked, looking Marc up and down. "You don't look it. Your hair is dark and you speak Italian."

"I was born in Belgium, but I have an English passport." Marc never missed an opportunity to grab onto the lifeline of that precious document. He hadn't yet fully realized that his cherished shield had been transformed into a dragon that could swallow him up at any minute.

"So, you are English then. You lot don't look so good now. You sail off nice and easy the lot of you, leaving your poor French friends in trouble. We Italians don't behave like that with our friends."

"What do you mean?" Alessandro was unable to control himself, leaping to his feet, upsetting his half-filled cup of barley coffee. "Italy has behaved like the villainous General Maramaldo, declaring war on a country that was already on its knees. France will capitulate in days. Is that what you call good behavior?"

"Shut up," his mother hissed at him, attempting to catch the policeman's eye with a tight smile. "He's just a kid. He talks nonsense most of the time."

Who the hell was Maramaldo? The officer chewed it over

in his head: it had to be an insult. Mixing with people like this was bad news. Faced with a citizen of an enemy state, he started boiling over with a rising sense of hostility. It wasn't them; it was himself he hated. He hadn't been able to summon the appropriate revulsion for these people, who looked to him like next-door neighbors. He locked the cell back up with an exaggerated clanging and didn't show his face again. He sent the skinny young agent with the bovine stare to call them to the chief's office.

The chief was not very tall but wiry and sported a well-trimmed mustache. He was speaking intently to Osvaldo and the man he had brought with him. He greeted the Rimons by raising his eyes for a fleeting moment from the papers scattered all over his desk. He then pointed vaguely at the chairs that been set out for them.

"This is Dr. Ferrando." Osvaldo introduced the man sitting next to him in a hurried and low voice, saving the explanation of his role for a later date. "Arrived in Italy at a date after 1919." The chief continued to peer over the papers. "Shouldn't you have been expelled under the 1938 Laws?"

Osvaldo looked at his brother-in-law, a concerned eyebrow raised, but Marc answered calmly. "The expulsion papers were retracted because my wife and son are Italian."

"We know, we know." The chief was growing irritated. "We already discussed this with these two gentlemen before you came in."

The verdict was already written: internment. With forced courtesy, the chief handed Marc a list of possible locations from which he was to choose one.

Marc glanced at the list quickly. "Far away," he said. "I want to go as far away from all this as possible."

The chief looked up. Nobody had ever asked anything of the kind; if anything, they pleaded for the opposite.

"When a Jew is banished, he leaves for good. He doesn't want to go and settle a stone's throw from where he lived before."

Marc spoke almost as if he were in a dream and those who knew him were amazed. He was usually so reserved; he had never identified as a Jew and would never have spoken about himself that way in front of people he didn't know.

A few minutes later, he came back to earth. He was absorbed by the list. There was the name of a small town in the Marches that reminded him of something. That's what it was: the hometown of Giustina, the housekeeper that used to work for the Passigli family, the cousins who were now known as "the ones whose son ran away." Owing to the Racial Laws, she had had to move to another city, but when she lived with the Passiglis, she would always regale visitors with stories of the wonderful fresh air in that tiny place up in the mountains where it was eternally spring. Seeing the name of that place in an official document of the Italian State was like spotting a familiar face in an anonymous crowd.

"Are you sure?" The chief continued to feel put out. There were people in high places who had this foreigner's back it seemed. He had better do things by the book. "Perhaps you were joking before? This place is really in the middle of nowhere."

Marc nodded his assent, almost as if he wanted to keep a hold on the only form of freedom he'd been accorded. Osvaldo looked disconcertedly at Emilia. He was hoping somebody would come to the rescue.

"Can we at least wait until the end of school for our son?" Emilia asked, keeping her voice level. "There are not many days left now," she added, primly.

"Ma'am, it is my duty to inform you that you and your son, as Italian citizens, are under no obligation to follow your for- eign husband."

"I know that," Emilia snapped testily.

"Do I take it that you are planning to leave together then?"

"Of course!" Her tone conveyed both impatience and astonishment.

The following day, on their release, they all three found themselves locked into Wanda's embraces. "Come over to ours, come over to ours," she repeated again and again as if her invitation could somehow make up for everything they had endured. Except for their cousin Carlo, the Communist who had been thrown into a cell every time a Fascist leader came to the city, nobody else in the family had ever been to prison. With a child in tow, it was unheard of.

When they got to Wanda and Osvaldo's house, they found Luigi sitting at the table, perfectly composed. Had he spent this time there, they inquired. No, he explained, he'd been fine at home on his own.

Before sitting at the table, Marc asked his brother-in-law in a whisper, "Who is this Dr. Ferrando?"

"Forget it," Osvaldo answered, waving his hand in the air. "He was just someone who could give us a hand."

Wanda managed to hold back until fruit was served at the end of the meal, and then she burst out with it. "Why did you choose to go to mad old Giustina's hometown? It's miles away; none of us has ever been there."

Marc went on peeling his apple carefully. Emilia made an agonized face at her sister. She had to let her sister know her husband had been the one to choose the place, not her.

"Okay," Wanda sighed. "They've given you until the end of the school year. What about next September?" What were they planning to do about their boy's studies?

"After the summer, Alessandro will come and stay here with you." Emilia's tone had gone back to being conciliatory. She was just a little irritated by all these questions piling up, those uttered as well as those not. It was a simple matter. Things happen, and families should behave according to the most elementary conventions.

Wanda wasn't listening any longer. She felt guilty, so guilty, but she couldn't do anything to stop her heart from leaping. A son-like nephew living with her in her house, day after day, month after month, for the fall, winter, spring . . . getting up in the morning and going to bed at night . . .

Chapter 30

A tiny, sleepy, solitary train station. The only thing that betrayed any human presence was a pot of dusty basil on a windowsill and a light ting-a-ling of a bell in the distance. They clambered onto a country bus that rattled through the valley for many miles before letting them off at the foot of a hill where the town was nestled. The only way to get there was by mule.

A stone wall ran along the main road up from the valley. There were cultivated fields and a chain of mountains in the distance. The sky was light blue and the air was crisp.

"So, this is Giustina's eternal spring!" It was the first time in months that Marc had smiled. "This is fine now, but I don't think this bracing air will be quite so welcome in the winter."

But Alessandro and even Emilia, affected by the timelessness of the landscape with valleys and mountains disappearing into the distance, were dumbstruck.

The accommodations were simple but not miserable. There were heavy wooden shutters, freshly-painted dark brown. The owner of the house, a rugged-looking man named Venanzio with lively eyes set in a face lined with deep wrinkles, greeted them in a gruff but friendly manner. Marc felt a seed of understanding being planted between them in that very first meeting. He was sure the man was an anti-Fascist; he had no idea who had pulled the strings, but somebody knew, and had suggested he take this house.

They spoke little; a few practical matters, that's all. Emilia couldn't help telling him about the bombs that had rained down on the naval fleet a few days before they left Genoa. "I'd never seen anything like it. It was terrible. Talk about a grand farewell from our city!"

Marc felt the need to intervene. "It was the first attack Italy has had from the sea."

"Paris fell the same day," Venanzio murmured. That sealed it for Marc. What would a peasant with a face cooked by the sun know about the catastrophes taking place in distant foreign cities?

Far away from everything. That day in the chief's office Marc had appeared to be in the grips of delirium, but he had done the right thing. There were no newspapers up there, and the war might as well have not existed except for the rivers of tears when mothers and young fiancées sent their young men off to fight. But these scenes were a mere repetition of the previous waves of emigration, when the men had set off with bundles on their backs to seek their fortune.

Alessandro was always surrounded by the local kids. He followed them blackberry picking, clambering up rocks in a continuous challenge as to who was the bravest, or kicking a ball around in a clearing full of thistles.

As evening drew in, they would sit on the ground in front of the tufa houses and play cards or Monopoly, with the set Alessandro had brought in his suitcase. A girl with a long braid down to her waist fell in love with him and followed him around like a puppy. She was twelve, her name was Benedetta, and she sang in the church choir. He had other thoughts spinning around his head, though. All the kids he used to play with in the courtyard—Giamba, Nino, Vittorio, and Salvatore who delivered ice to his house—knew he was Jewish, but they didn't care. They were his friends, no questions asked. That's why he loved them. The kids up here in the mountain had no clue that

Jews existed, no idea what they were. There was no discrimination here to deal with: quite simply the problem had never come about. Alessandro felt a weightless as the air that filled his lungs. The feeling of being outside the ghetto made him light-headed. It felt as if he were spreading his wings and flying into a universe with no connotations: no nation, no age, no gender, no religion, just a collection of human beings.

At night in his room he would sometimes take out the box where he kept Nonna Rachele's Star of David pendant in two shades of gold, and he would slide it between his hands. But it was just an old habit that reminded him of life before this.

"The only reason we're here is that when he was young your father chose the wrong passport." Emilia had translated Alessandro's feeling into her own words. She wanted to convince her son that being Jewish had nothing whatsoever to do with the fact that they had been sent to the mountains. In her view, in short, it was best not to mention the little detail around town so as not to complicate things. It appeared that, despite everything, she was content to be there. The wife of the pharmacist had invited her over for a hibiscus cordial, which the woman had poured out from a jug that may even have been silver. Other women said hello to her, and some had started confiding in her with the local gossip. As far as the house was concerned, she was better off here than in Rome.

Not that she was behind this improvement. It had gone like this. Maria, Venanzio's sister, came almost every day to take care of and clean the house. She had been doing it for years, and nobody had asked her to stop, even though her brother was now lodging with her after renting out his own house. She often happened to prepare their meals, too: there were certain vegetables she foraged that only she knew how to cook.

The laws that forbade people to work as domestics in Jewish households, Emilia thought to herself, had never reached this place. In any case, they weren't paying Maria. After two months, Marc said they should give her something, and Maria accepted the envelope with very good grace. On the first day of rain, she quickly lit the fire; nobody in the family would have known how, Emilia realized equally quickly. When she wrote to Wanda, wary of censorship, she only ever mentioned a kind woman who came occasionally to help around the house. Wanda exclaimed to her husband, "Lucky her! My sister has found herself a maid."

The lack of newspapers was the only thing that made Marc restless and agitated. However, in Venanzio and Maria's house there was a radio. Increasingly often, Marc would sit at his landlord's table with a glass of wine and listen. They heard on the radio that France had surrendered and signed an armistice in the very same spot where Germany had had to accept the humiliating treaty after the First World War that had led to such suffering for the German people. When he got home, Marc told Alessandro, "You were right back in prison when you said they were behaving like Maramaldo, flogging a dead horse. Italy declared war on France twelve days before it capitulated. Now they can demand a little piece of land near Ventimiglia."

His wife said, "Leave him alone. Can't you see the boy is finally thinking about something else?" After a pause, she muttered, "You should do the same," and reminded him that he'd had a heart attack. Since arriving in the mountains, his health had improved drastically. Marc thought perhaps he should be thankful to the Fascist government for taking care of his well-being.

Marc also managed to think about other things. He would go out in the evenings and play cards in the tavern. There, too, was a table, a flask of wine, a pale lamp hanging from the ceiling. It felt as if he were back home with Osvaldo and their father-in-law.

Until recently, two English women had been interned in the town, but they had asked to be transferred. They were sisters who were both painters. People in the town said one of them copied the other's paintings. They could see the women were foreign, but the man playing cards with them didn't seem to be foreign at all. Only when he lost, he'd curse in Genoese dialect, but Genoa was still Italy.

Emilia asked him from time to time, "What do your friends in the town say? Has Venanzio ever been married?"

"He might be a widower, but they don't talk about him much; they say they don't know either," Marc would answer vaguely. He thought his landlord must have a secret lover somewhere, but he didn't tell his wife that.

Summer was coming to an end. After every rain shower, Maria came over to light the fire even though Marc had learned to do it perfectly. After a long correspondence with Osvaldo and Wanda, they decided to send Alessandro off on the train by himself. Someone in the town would take him to the mule track, and then he would ride the bus to the station. However, surprising them all, Osvaldo turned up. He sat straight in the saddle, as composed as if he were on a triumphal round of the race course after winning a horse show. He was wearing a white summer suit with a rust-red pin-striped shirt under it and a matching pocket square.

His wife had insisted, he explained in a rush. Their nephew was not grown up enough for such a long journey, and what if the train were bombed?

Marc was happier than anyone to see Osvaldo. They had so many things to talk about since they'd last had the chance. The only person he could discuss politics with was his silent landlord, Venanzio; it was best not to go overboard with his son, after all. Osvaldo started right away: Italy declaring war on France in the final two minutes, when it was on its last legs; it

hadn't gained more than two feet of land in the Alps, just a little strip of coastline right by the border, but it had been given
a seat at the negotiating table, that was true. They both knew
all this, but they needed to pick up the game of commenting
together from where they had left off.

"That Venanzio chap is an interesting character," Osvaldo
said.

He had been invited to drink a glass of wine and listen to
the radio with them. "He never says a word but he's aware of
everything. I think he must be one of us."

A half-smile escaped Marc's lips. He was almost positive
that even if the Racial Laws had never been made, Osvaldo
would have always been an anti-Fascist, even if he couldn't
quite see him as a militant opponent.

CHAPTER 31

N onno Luigi wandered around the room restlessly, out of sorts.

"He says he wants to go back to his own house," Wanda confided to her nephew, "but he doesn't have *his own house*, he lives with you, right?"

"He's lived there for nine years. His life is there now," Alessandro murmured.

His grandfather was berating him, too. "If only you were still a child, I'd have the excuse to take you out and go out myself," he huffed, staring grimly at the boy's grown body as if it were a newfound enemy.

"Go out anyway." The retort slipped out; he knew his grandfather hated easy answers.

"I was less bored at the madwoman's house." Alessandro took a while to realize the "madwoman" had to be his mother. He nearly burst out laughing. He wouldn't have called her "mad." Malicious, maybe.

"Aren't you happy with Aunt Wanda? She's nice to everybody," Alessandro tried to argue.

"Didn't you hear me? I'm bored. At least with your mother there was never a dull moment; we had to be alert at all times to her moods, guess which side of the bed she had gotten out of, line up our defenses. That is living, too." Luigi sighed with a false expression of remorse on his face. "With Wanda nothing ever happens. I know exactly how she'll react, what answer she'll give, I can even predict her exclamations."

"It's fine for me. I'm happy here." Alessandro looked around the room, at the curtains, the armchairs, and the bookshelf that had a gap where the radio had lived before it was confiscated yet emanated no sense of sadness.

"You wish Wanda were your mother. I've known that for a while. If you think about it, though, you'll realize Wanda is an ordinary, small-minded little woman."

So? Aunt Wanda was kind, she liked taking care of him, she took part in his life without suffocating him too much: what else could he hope for? Who said that your mother had to be better than everyone else, anyway? If anything, parents want their children to tussle for the top spot in the agony of life, but the opposite doesn't make sense. In fact, it often spells trouble.

He thought of his mother striding into every room just after six in the morning, whatever the weather (especially when Cesarina worked for them), and loudly throwing the windows wide open. If anybody dared complain, she would retort, "Houses need to be kept clean."

"I like it here," Alessandro said again, digging his heels in.

Anyway, it wasn't true that his aunt didn't have a mind of her own. He remembered when they'd followed *The Four Musketeers* together and when she'd started listening to the radio on her own, capturing the first signals of a campaign against Jews and growing alarmed. Nobody had understood at the time why she was so upset. And yet, the "ordinary small-minded little woman" had understood the truth long before the rest of them.

Nonno Luigi's mood darkened. He knew, because he'd seen her one evening, the look in Wanda's eyes when she watched her nephew sleeping through the half-closed door.

Osvaldo was happy to be able to discuss things with his nephew; a little, at least. His brother-in-law was far away and, in order to be able to talk about current affairs—with an extra dose of confidential detail here and there—he had to be content with what he had. The invasion of Greece that Italy was convinced would be a walk in the park, but turned out to be a disaster, a counter-attack culminating in Italy's defeat and subsequent retreat into Albania. Mussolini had not informed his allies of his plans, hoping to present them with a fait accompli—a victory already in his war chest—and now he was going to have to call them in to help. It was well known that the Germans wouldn't be too happy about it, as Greece was not in their plan.

"What do you bet," Uncle Osvaldo laughed, "that thanks to Italy, Germany is more likely to lose the war after this latest escapade?

Alessandro listened attentively, at times even excitedly, but he was still a boy.

"You know I've always admired your father for his wisdom, but this rash decision . . . he must have been off his head!" The expression came up often in their conversations and, whenever it did, Osvaldo would shake his own head.

"Now that it's winter up there on the tip of an ice block, in the most neglected corner of Italy where night falls straight after lunch, they're beginning to realize things are not so great!"

"Well, he's interned; he can't change anything now," Alessandro retorted once.

"Oh yes he can," Osvaldo said, his voice rumbling like thunder. His lips curled into a smile: he loved being the first person to break important news. "Your father has been persuaded. He's applied for a transfer."

They all discussed the move at dinner, including Wanda and Nonno Luigi. The town he had applied for was nearer to them, between Liguria and Piedmont. "You'll be able to go every weekend, not only for the summer vacation. You can even get there by train," Osvaldo explained to his nephew.

Wanda fixed her eye on another point in the room. "That vase over there," she said vaguely after a while, "I must get around to cleaning it. It doesn't even look like crystal anymore."

Her husband answered, "Come on, we'll all be getting on that train."

There were still several months to go, at least until the end of the summer; maybe September was the most likely date. If the parents were about to move closer to home, what would be the point of undertaking a long journey all the way to the Marches once Alessandro finished school? The logic was impeccable; Wanda was particularly sold.

Seeking them out one by one in plenty of time, Wanda had managed to procure all the ingredients she needed. For her nephew's birthday she would present, triumphantly, the most enviable cake with fourteen colored candles.

They lived within the system; fine. Injustice was the main feature that shaped their lives, but they had all grown used to it. It was the endless series of vexatious, petty, little injustices— the pinches that kept him awake when he was dying to fall asleep—that made Alessandro quiver with rage.

The Genoa Jewish school was not recognized by the education board; in June, even when there were no state exams, Jewish students had to sit end-of-year tests with other pupils from private schools in a public school. "With," of course, was not the right term. The Jewish kids had to wait outside while the Aryans sat their tests, and they were not allowed in before the janitor had checked all the classrooms and corridors to make sure no "pure-blooded" students might be contaminated.

That summer, with all the uncertainty regarding what would happen once his parents returned, Alessandro felt the oppression more harshly.

They were let in during what would have been the lunch

hour; they were all sweaty. The head teacher, Castorina, with black hair and a beard worthy of the Risorgimento, was waiting for them at the door of the classroom with his arm raised in a Fascist salute. The others, with differing degrees of cooperation, all did the same. Alessandro didn't lift his arm.

"You?" Castorina barked. "Why aren't you saluting?"

"I can't give a Fascist salute because I'm not a Fascist."

"What do you mean you're not a Fascist?" The head teacher was startled; he'd never heard a response of that kind.

Alessandro, by contrast, was at peace with himself. He didn't want to provoke the man, he was just explaining his reason.

"You should be happy. You wrote it in your Manifesto: 'Jews cannot enroll in the Fascist Party.' Mine is simply an act of obedience in the name of the Racial Laws." There was not a hint of irony in that stupid boy's voice. The head teacher almost felt humiliated by him.

"Go to your place," he said, looking the other way. At the end of the exam, he reminded himself to lower the mark on the Italian paper Alessandro had just handed in.

While they were having dinner, the telephone rang. "It's for you," Wanda said to Alessandro returning from the corridor looking astonished. "They say it's the school."

"This is Professor Brenda. I was at school this morning when your group came in for the test. Your answer created quite a discussion in the teacher's room today." Alessandro heard him chuckling. "Usually answers like that don't go unpunished, but in this case, there was no chance of objecting. They are the ones declaring you're the enemy and all you could do was take note."

Alessandro felt awkward. He would have liked to laugh with the teacher, but he thought it would be too familiar. "Can you get a paper and pen?" the teacher asked him.

Alessandro came back to the phone with a notebook and a

pencil. Professor Brenda dictated all the questions that would be on the history test the next day. He did the same every day for every subject.

On the last day, Gaetano Brenda asked him to write down his home address. "Come and see me. I'd like to have a chat with you. We know one another from school already, right?"

Actually, he'd had to ask the janitor which of the teachers was Professor Brenda although he was sure he would have worked it out eventually. The teacher was a little stooped, his head hanging slightly, but it wasn't age that had curved him, just habit. It was as if he wanted to peer at you from his own particular perspective.

CHAPTER 32

Professor Brenda had called him again to invite him over to his house. Alessandro accepted right away even though that day . . .

Alma was due to leave at exactly the same time, and he wanted to say goodbye. He had noticed that she was excited by, and grudgingly admiring, of his fight with the head teacher before their exams. She had told him he was "intelligent and brave," but Alessandro had been disappointed as he felt her praise was more appropriate for a teacher than for someone in love (although he knew perfectly well Alma wasn't in love with him). Perhaps if they had a chance to meet up before she left, she would mention the episode again and choose different words.

Of all their school friends, Alma was the only one leaving for a summer vacation. She had a grandmother who was almost rich and almost Catholic. Her Nonna Rosina had been widowed early, and had re-married an industrialist who was not Jewish. With her Aryan surname, Rosina could swan around spending her summers in a villa on the Versilia coast. Alma had been invited to join her and was leaving that day. She would not be seeing her school friends until the fall. It was hard to imagine what they would have talked about anyway.

Professor Brenda, his head tilted slightly to one side in an expression of sympathy, had described what he had done that day as a courageous political action. This made Alessandro feel uneasy. When he had answered back to the head teacher that day, he hadn't considered it the ardent anti-Fascist reaction everyone else seemed to stubbornly see it as; all he had been doing was making a logical argument and drawing the logical conclusion from that argument. The Fascists should have been pleased with his obedience, rather than requiring those they had thrown out with such alacrity to join their rank and file. That was it. At least, he thought that was it, but when he explained this to Professor Brenda, the older man smiled. "You'd be a perfect agit-prop," he chuckled. They were sitting on two worn-out armchairs, one of which had lost its springs; there were books everywhere, some even piled up on the floor. It was all part of the script. Alessandro had been expecting it. In the other room there must have been a cat. Every now and again, he heard it meowing, seemingly in protest, but the teacher didn't take any notice,

He asked, "How old are you? And Alessandro answered, "Fifteen in February."

"It's June, and there are eight months to go before next February. Does saying the word 'fourteen' horrify you for some reason?"

Gaetano Brenda burst into a loud belly laugh.

Alessandro was amazed to find himself telling him why he had started school early and how he had always been condemned to being in class with boys who were older than him.

"And girls, I imagine." Professor Brenda had imagined correctly. Alessandro suddenly felt like pouring out his whole life to the lanky teacher slouching in his armchair. And so he did.

That his father was a "political exile" impressed Professor Brenda no end, and Alessandro didn't have the courage to correct him: his father was an exile but not a political one.

"Did you know that the Germans have invaded the Soviet Union without declaring war officially?" the teacher asked, changing the subject quickly, to Alessandro's surprise, disappointment even. Of course, he answered. They'd discussed it for the whole evening with his Uncle Osvaldo. They were convinced the Russians would stop them.

Professor Brenda was sure, too, but how could one be sure these days?

"History is already written. Good will always win over Evil. We can have no illusions about how or when it will happen, however." The man sighed. He suddenly looked extremely sad and extremely old. Then, at point-blank range, with a flash of mockery in his eyes, he fired off his question: "Are you a Communist?"

"My cousin is a Communist, he was a railway worker, but now he isn't, isn't a railway worker I mean, but he's still a Communist." Alessandro was consumed by self-hatred. In his confused, childish answer he could detect the mark his mother had branded him with. The more he tried to rise to the occasion the more befuddled he became. Professor Brenda didn't seem to notice. "With young people like you," he said slowly, "we'll be able to conquer the monster that is trying to suffocate and destroy the whole of Europe. We'll succeed. But then?" Society can't survive if the weak are oppressed; we cannot build anything on a foundation of injustice. In no time at all, there will be new Fascists and new Nazis. Everyone should be able to work with the skills they have and receive what they need. This is what we need to fight for. It's the only way the world will be different. Gaetano Brenda looked spellbound; he was staring at Alessandro but appeared not to see him. "In the Soviet Union this dream is coming true. Class privileges have been swept away," Brenda said with a dramatic gesture of his hand. Then he went dark in the face. "The country is in grave danger now, it needs the support of people who believe in our values," he murmured. He was back with his feet on the ground now; the student in his room was so young that he was almost embarrassed. "Do you agree?" he asked the boy. "I can see you hate injustice. That's why we're here talking about it."

Alessandro didn't feel he'd been forced in any way. Being called a Communist gave him a thrill of pride. While he was listening to the teacher, his mind had wandered to his group of courtyard friends, Giamba, Salvatore and the others. He saw them less often now that he lived with his uncle and aunt, and they all had jobs now. He'd like to see them one day governing his country. They'd never asked him whether he was born in Jerusalem. They'd never laughed at him like the kids at his school had done. Ever.

Standing by the front door, the teacher asked him when his parents would be back. "End of September, I think." The boy looked distracted.

"You'll be happy to see them, won't you?"

"Of course."

Gaetano Brenda had never heard such an uncertain "of course."

Professor Brenda had left for the summer, too. He had a married daughter and a grandchild in another city; he and his wife were spending their vacation with the family. Alessandro was embarrassed to hear these personal, everyday details of his life: the figure of a mentor should be as ungraspable as that of a rabbi. He had only ever seen the rabbi's children from far off.

Before leaving, Alessandro had had the opportunity to ask him, "What can I do for . . . ?" For Communism, for the struggle against injustice . . . he didn't feel he could use these consecrated words. He had stopped short at "for . . ." but Brenda had understood. "Nothing sensational for now; you're only fourteen," the teacher said, stressing the word "fourteen". "Study, think, try and keep yourself well informed, try and circulate your ideas among kids of your age. That's already a lot, you know."

Over that summer vacation that had been canceled on the basis of an agreement between his parents and his aunt and uncle, Alessandro took German and English lessons in the whitewashed building of the Sisters of Charity of Nevers. These sharp nuns were his first political conquests. He started by bringing them a carefully wrapped gift—like fresh eggs in sheets of newspaper—of the latest news from Radio London. He got the news from Uncle Osvaldo who went to a friend's house to tune in. Ostensibly, his friend was a hotshot Fascist, but knowing how things really stood during a war could be useful for everyone. The nuns couldn't get enough of it.

He was then quick to hone in on the Soviet Union. The nuns were sympathetic to the focus of Communism on the rights of the working poor. They soon returned to the subject of the war, however. The counter-attack on Hitler's troops had unfortunately failed; the Yugoslavian partisan insurrection under Tito, who was strongly supported by Stalin, had been exhilarating; days later, the official alliance between the Soviets and the Brits had heralded new hope. The nuns listened to their young disciple singing his epic tale. Comparing stories from Radio London, they pinned colored flags showing the relative positions of the different armies on a giant map they had on their wall.

He saw them from far off. They were standing there, a suitcase in hand, in front of the police check-point at the station. Of course! They were no ordinary travelers; they were internees on one leg of their journey. They could only stay in Genoa until the connecting train arrived that would take them to the town written on their travel permits. Alessandro didn't move. They hadn't noticed him yet. From a distance, they didn't look like his father, with his detached indulgence, and his mother, with her perennially pervasive rancor; they were just two figures, two insignificant dots lost in the meaningless machinations of the universe. The fact that they had been deprived of their home city at the precise moment they arrived in it no longer felt like an injustice. Rather, it was simply one more of the contradictions in the comedy of paradoxes.

He moved a little, and they came into focus. He was ashamed at having perceived his father, who so persistently tried to help him grow up, and his mother, who so cherished the idea of destroying his chances at it, as one and the same thing.

His father's face was less tense than before, almost relaxed. He noticed as he was hugging him. His uncle was right: their internment in the mountains had been a cure for his parents' health. Osvaldo and Wanda confirmed his impression when they came running to meet them. They talked all at once, not stopping until it was time for his parents to get on their next train. Their goodbyes were hasty and light-hearted. School had already begun, but Alessandro would go and see them the following Saturday.

"We might come, too," his aunt trilled, but his uncle said, "Let them be, just the three of them. We'll go another time."

"But she asked me," Wanda, humiliated, pointed towards her sister.

CHAPTER 33

M arc had found out that the Carabinieri sergeant was the same age as him and remembered tales from the front in the First World War. Another coincidence: Sergeant Egisto Capriotti was from the Marches, and when he saw where they had traveled from, he was extremely pleased. From the start, he was cordial, almost as if they'd been neighbors. He had many points going in his favor, but that was no reason to let their guard down.

"Why does he have to come around every evening to check up on me?" Marc vented to Alessandro. "Where does he think I could go, out in the boondocks like this?"

Marc and his wife—with an unusual level of agreement—started calling the place where they were now interned "the boondocks" from the very first day. Perhaps because they were expecting something a little better in their own region, the house never felt like home. Perhaps, too, the faraway town in the Marches where they had stayed (and where nobody ever came to check upon them) was already tinged with the indulgently rosy colors of memory.

This new town was not a vacation destination: it was neither up in the mountains nor by the sea, and all it had to offer was an age-old agricultural economy and small family businesses producing lime. The people were taciturn. Marc and Emilia interpreted their reserve as hostility. A bald man of no apparent age would cycle up and down the dusty streets and people kept out of his way. Rumor had it that he was a Fascist spy.

Seeing his son every weekend, and his in-laws nearly as often, was the greatest possible compensation for Marc. There was one other advantage, however. A radio.

The house he rented had a big set made of chestnut-colored briar root, which sat on a specially made table. Marc had moved the table and radio to the bedroom to protect it, so that nobody would bump into it, he claimed. In the quiet evenings he would go straight to the bedroom and tune in to Radio London, prepared and eager to be enflamed by the news. When Alessandro was there, he sat next to him on the bed and was exhilarated alongside him.

"Wasn't there a radio in this house?" the sergeant asked on one of his evening incursions. "Yes, there was," they answered. They'd taken it into the bedroom in case it got damaged in any way. Egisto Capriotti was a man who'd clearly been tested by life. The impish expression on his face didn't fit his character. "What time do you listen to Radio London?" he whispered.

Marc denied it hotly, defending himself, waving his arms around like a southerner, but a calm voice stopped him in his tracks. "I need to know the precise time because I want to come and listen, too."

Since that day, the sergeant was never a minute late.

It was December. The first snow fall covered the lime dust. Everyone had heard the news, not only those listening to Radio London. Japan had launched an attack and sunk six battleships from the US Navy fleet anchored at Pearl Harbor, without so much as a declaration of war. The following day, the United States declared war on Japan. It only took three days for Germany and Italy to be proclaimed officially at war with America.

"They've got a nerve," Osvaldo joked. "If someone in the Italian government had picked up a New York telephone directory, they would have seen there were more names than words in our dictionary and that might have knocked a bit of sense in to them!" The comment wasn't his: he'd picked it up from one of his acquaintances and never tired of repeating it. A few months before, the Americans had been in a position to lend a billion dollars to the Soviet Union to help them defend themselves.

"Doesn't your aunt ever sew your buttons back on?" his mother asked when she saw a button hanging off his shirt. Her tone wasn't bitter. She had begun to accept, with some degree of gratitude, that her sister had played a maternal role towards her son. They were no longer forced to meet during the weekends. Emilia had not been interned herself; she could now take a train and go into Genoa to see her family whenever she wanted. It didn't happen often. Alessandro was relieved. He had been terribly worried that his life would have to change yet again.

Nonno Luigi was harsh in his criticism. "So, you don't like the mother you have?" he'd say. "Show some muscle, boy. Wage war with her. You can't just switch her for a nicer one."

It was easy for him to judge. For a long time now, his life had shrunk down to the immediate family circle. That was not the case for Alessandro. His problems with his mother could easily sink into the background, as far as he was concerned. There were other uncertainties to concern himself with. There was Alma, who may well admire him but almost certainly didn't love him, even though he'd grown a good bit taller in the meantime (he was still younger than her). At school, he'd run into Rabbi Bonfiglioli occasionally. He wasn't their Jewish Culture teacher, but he would come into their class every now and again and sit down to take the lesson. Alessandro would often recall the day of his bar mitzvah when the rabbi had said "You'll be a good Jew" and he'd felt really uneasy. He'd never gone back to synagogue since. Only at Yom Kippur, like everyone, or when his little cousin had his circumcision ceremony at eight days old. He wondered whether the rabbi even remembered saying it. When he analyzed a Bible passage in class, the rabbi would look at him and act pleased when he gave a good answer. He knew just how much value Rabbi Bonfiglioli placed on studying. "Better to close a synagogue than a school," was the motto he liked to repeat.

He would have liked to tell him that he'd become a Communist and discuss it with him, because he felt Communism had some points in common with Judaism, but the opportunity for a one-on-one conversation never presented itself. He had talked about Marxism with his father, who didn't seem to disapprove of his meetings with Professor Brenda. Nonetheless, he felt Marc was both wary and skeptical. Stalin was an evil dictator, who had systematically gotten rid of everyone who overshadowed him in any way, including many army generals. He had created a vacuum, his father had said, and now that the country was at war their absence spelled trouble. Alessandro was divided: he believed his father, but he also believed that he was not sufficiently aware of the sacrifices needed to make a revolution.

His father was entangled in other matters. One evening he had suddenly brought up the subject of Nello Rosselli, who had been murdered by Mussolini's thugs years before, and who had declared at a youth conference Marc happened to have been at that political engagement and the struggle for freedom were the only ways one could play a role as a Jew. There was a great deal to think about; perhaps this should be "their" way forward. When Alessandro surfaced from this turmoil of permanently contradictory thoughts, his grandfather banging on about waging war on his mother felt absurd. As if to prove his point, Nonno Luigi waged his own war with his daughter, who had gone straight back to her non-stop nagging. "Whatever do you need to go back to the house for? The concierge has the keys and she keeps it clean," she would harp on. "You won't feel safe if there's always someone coming and going."

"I go and water the plants," he would answer proudly. "She never remembers to do it."

At which Emilia would mutter under her breath, "He's always spilling water all over the floor. Why on earth doesn't he water the plants here?"

Emilia also disapproved of the heavy food her father ate, which in her view was unsuitable for a man of his age. Her sister would answer mildly, "We're not in the countryside where you can get anything that grows in the fields. We have to be happy with what we can get with our ration cards."

Luigi would deliberately challenge his daughter, looking straight at her as he sunk his teeth into a raw onion.

At Professor Brenda's house, Alessandro had met a young Marxist, with a head of hair like a lion's mane and thick spectacles that had gotten him off active duty. He would oppose any attempt advanced by anybody elsewhere on the political spectrum at being pragmatic, or opening a constructive dialogue, with a resounding "No." He had most certainly mistaken stubbornness for idealism. In his presence, Alessandro was unable to discuss with Brenda the doubts his father had raised.

"God is on the wrong side," Wanda moaned in anguish. "That lot is on a winning streak." For her, "that lot" were the Germans and the Italians, recently joined by the Japanese. Dispatches from the Far East, Cyrenaica, and Stalingrad only announced good news from the "wrong side." Even the exiled Jewish writer, Stefan Zweig, had been so convinced the Nazis were about to win the war that he'd committed suicide with his wife in a remote Brazilian jungle.

"God doesn't take the tram," Luigi pronounced one evening at dinner. They all stared at him. The old man had continued to take as his model his wife's passion for Jewish popular wisdom expressed in proverbs, and, every now and again, he would make up a few of his own. What I mean is, God is in no hurry, he explained, irritated at not being understood. 1942, the year Alessandro finally turned fifteen, was truly bleak and ominous.

Towards the end of the year, however, God perhaps had gotten to the right stop: the tram was finally running in the opposite direction.

As an unusually mild October came to a close, the victorious second battle of El Alamein broke the Axis's lucky streak. A thrilling sequence of events followed: the Anglo-American invasion of French Morocco and Algeria; Soviet forces breaking through the German front besieging Stalingrad. Soon after, the Germans were forced to withdraw from the Caucasus and, even more disastrously, the Italian divisions were completely routed, if not annihilated.

At Aunt Wanda's house—as in many other houses—people began to stick their noses out the door and look up at the sky, even though the sky was often occupied, too. Literally hundreds of bombs were dropped on Genoa and other northern Italian cities in the air raids, darkening the firmament as they dropped.

Alessandro is at a friend's, studying all night because they have an extra test tomorrow. The intermittent, funereal air-raid sirens start wailing at ten in the evening. They're not worried. The planes have flown over their heads many times before, only to continue elsewhere. This time, there is a violent blast followed by more angry, closer crashing sounds. The walls of the house shake, as if they are begging for mercy. The two boys, his friend's parents, and the other inhabitants of the building gather on the stairs and, as the sky turns red, run like crazy to the shelter. It's in a tunnel dug into the mountains right in the middle of the city, the long corridors of bare rock-face affording protection to the human beings cowering there. Alessandro relaxes. In the deep belly of the earth, he feels a sense of safety—of eternity—pervading his spirit. As eternal as the hours they spend there. British and American bombers take turns, dancing a relentless hoedown, until four in the morning when the silence that falls is more unsettling than the clamor before. When they emerge, the whole city is in flames. The incendiary bombs designed to reinforce the effect of the explosive bombs have done their job. Genoa looks like a circle of hell, burning in every fiber of its being.

Alessandro looks around, horrified, and then starts running through the city streets, dodging crumbling cornices, still ablaze, that fall without warning onto the paving stones. Piazza della Vittoria is on fire, as is the train station at Brignole. There is not one spot as far as the eye can see that has not been licked by the flames. Home. Is the house where his aunt and uncle, his grandfather, and every now and again his mother live still standing? Where are they? The thought hammering in his head takes his breath away. One street after another, a turn, and right at the end, through the clouds of smoke that are beginning to lift, he sees the house. Standing. The family is out on the street with a clutch of neighbors, all in coats over their pajamas. They have just come out of the air-raid shelter, which is the cellar in their building. They are waiting for him; not just the family, all of them. It is as if they were ashamed to return to their homes after surviving that great collective fire-storm.

They hug him; Wanda gets there first. Alessandro tears himself free. He's still gasping for breath. His face is flushed, his eyes flashing as if he were possessed.

"Give him some water, poor boy, he's terrified," the neighbors say in dialect. Alessandro takes the water but doesn't drink it. He splashes it on his face, bursting into laughter.

"They exist! They exist! They're coming!" he yells as loud

as he can. Has the boy lost his mind? People look puzzled. They don't get what he is saying. His uncle is the only one to look over at him quickly and grin.

"Don't you worry," a Fascist guard in uniform reassures him. "Our air defenses are the best in the world. Who knows how many of those dogs have been knocked out of the sky by our flak tonight."

CHAPTER 34

Alessandro no longer has that hallucinated look in his eyes. You can get used to the good as well as the bad. Hope now sits at their table almost every day and has no intention of giving up the seat it has just conquered. 1943 is advancing, brandishing the sword of an avenging angel.

The Red Army's final attack bringing the Stalingrad siege to an end, more frequent bombings of German territory (*territory!*), the British administration of Tripolitania, the withdrawal of Japanese forces from Guadalcanal island: it's a vast swath of the world that's being lacerated. The city of Cagliari bombed to almost total destruction. Does peace really require such a high price? There would be time to reflect later, not now while there are enemy forces out there willing to kill you and millions of others like you.

Sergeant Capriotti never misses an appointment to tune in to Radio London. If his body were able to express what he feels inside, he would be bouncing out of the house every time.

Alessandro continues to receive Radio London news from Uncle Osvaldo, but some carefully prepared items are sometimes broadcast on the official news. Increasingly, now, he runs straight to Gaetano Brenda's house. The wave of strikes in the factories of northern Italy make the professor euphoric. He no longer slouches; he soars. His young disciple with the lion-mane hair, however, never fails to talk him down: let's be cautious, let's look more carefully at their reasons, we can't unite forces with any old protest. Alessandro detests him. He always hopes he won't be there. He hopes to find the professor on his own, so he can talk to him in depth at least one more time, maybe to confide that he's caught between two mothers—one good and one bad—and that the bad one is his own.

And so one more year passes by and comes to an end. In June, just before the end of the semester, the Allies invade the island of Pantelleria, off Sicily. "They're in Italy already!" Alessandro says to his uncle. His uncle has just said the same thing to him, but it's nice to repeat news that gives you such joy. The mandatory external end-of-year exams take place in a different school from last year. Hopefully, there won't be a head teacher like Castorina with his Fascist salute. Alessandro is almost irritated by the memory of his "act of heroism," and Alma seems to have forgotten all about it. At least, she never mentions it when they walk home together after school.

For the vacation, Alessandro goes back to being Marc and Emilia's boy out in the boondocks. His aunt and uncle seem to like the place more and more. They have quite often rented a room in a nearby house and come to stay the night. Tuning in to Radio London with relatives is much more thrilling than listening to a Fascist giving the official news. They usually go back to the city the next day, however, as they can't leave Nonno Luigi on his own for too long, even though he always claims the days they are away are paradise.

Osvaldo had secretly brought Marc some gems to work on; clients who knew his brother-in-law's handiwork well had entrusted them to him. Picking up his work tools once again fills Marc with great joy. He's working, working again, earning something with his craft. They hardly spend any of their savings living up there in the countryside. Moreover, they receive a meager allowance—a laughable sum—from the state during their internment. The fact is, as his mother-in-law used to say, "Idle hands are the devil's workshop."

Emilia is somber. She doesn't want him to work, he's foreign, and his license has been taken away. She's scared he'll be found out. In any case, not working was good for his health.

Osvaldo thinks Emilia has a chip on her shoulder towards anyone who actually produces something. He could be wrong, however. She has waged a great deal on her son being a genius.

Radio London seems to have the function of gathering together all the most restless characters in the remote town. Alessandro is happy to tune in with his father in the bedroom and to have made friends with Sergeant Capriotti. He has a son, he says, but he's fighting in Russia.

July has come. The harvested fields are dry and prickly and there is not a breath of wind in the air. There's a young woman with curly hair in the town. Her husband has been away at the front for years and she needs another man to remind her of him. There is very little choice around there: the men are either very old or very young. She chooses the latter: a boy from the city who is unlikely to return to this town in the future. Alessandro gets back home looking dazed. His expression is the same as it was the day Genoa was bombed and burned to the ground.

"How on earth can you be late for dinner in a place like this?" Emilia complains. "There's never anything to do here."

"There are things to do; there certainly are," his uncle answers. He's the only one to guess what may have happened. Marc peers at his son, interrogating him with his eyes. He waits a while and then gives up.

"The U.S. Seventh and the British Eighth Army have invaded Sicily." The news explodes like a bomb; Marc, whose gestures were usually controlled, explodes, too. He hugs his son tight. The sergeant is suddenly at the door and calls Marc by his name for the first time, using the familiar *"tu."*

After the invasion and the bombing of Rome, with the Pope leaving the Vatican to bring comfort to the people in their crumbling homes, Italy was creaking, on the brink.

"Fascism is over! Mussolini is out!" someone shouts one evening in the boondocks. Doors and windows are thrown open. People fill the streets, including the old and infirm. The sergeant is at the Rimon's house, but he goes straight out into the square. Now, more than ever, he must keep order; there may well be personal vendettas. The mayor has already run away. The bald man on his bicycle, by contrast, is circling the town dizzily, without stopping. Maybe he's not a Fascist spy, after all.

Yes, it is true. The Grand Council of Fascism was responsible for doing away with Mussolini. It was as if a Great Storyteller had made the dreams of everyone who had been persecuted come true. The King had the *Duce* arrested, disbanded the Fascist Party, and the Fascist government buildings were closed. Power was handed over to the Marshal of Italy, Pietro Badoglio. The regime was over, notices saying "No dogs or Jews" were over, separate schools were over, head master Castorina's raised arm is paralyzed in a Fascist salute. Alessandro wonders which school Alma will go to.

"Egisto?" Marc turns to the sergeant. They are both on first-name terms now. "What about us? Can we go now?"

"No, Marco." The sergeant uses the Italian version of his name to underscore their friendship. "We're still at war, allies of Germany. You are still an enemy alien."

CHAPTER 35

T he sergeant has changed. Haven't you noticed?" Marc looked at his son, confused. "He's more reserved, less friendly." Could he, deep down, be missing the Fascists in some way?

"I don't know," Alessandro answered vaguely. "Maybe he just comes here less because he doesn't need Radio London anymore. National radio isn't Fascist now; they can speak more freely."

"He's getting cocky because now that the *podestà* has gone he's the one in charge," was Emilia's pronouncement.

"Don't you understand how much responsibility he has with everything so messed up right now?" was the point Osvaldo made when he was consulted. He carried on tuning into Radio London; Italian radio did not provide that much information on the war. Radio London addressed Italians directly now, exhorting them to put pressure on Badoglio to declare a cease-fire. "They've brought down the Fascist regime. Are they going to *bring down* the war too?" Osvaldo quipped, pulling the cheeky face of a kid planning a bit of mischief.

Sergeant Capriotti came around that evening. "It's no laughing matter," he muttered. "I can't imagine how the Germans would take a betrayal of the kind." Then he blurted, "I wonder if you know that the Germans are quietly creeping into the country from all sides. There's a steady flow in Ventimiglia alone."

It wasn't true that the sergeant was getting cocky; he was

simply worried. Marc had understood but it still made him sad. Since the fall of Fascism, Capriotti had never called him by his first name again.

Over that summer, Alessandro made a new friend. Tullio was the same age as him and boarded in a Jesuit school in Alessandria, Piedmont, during the school year. He only came back to his parents' house during the summer vacation. Unlike in the mountain town in the Marches region, here everyone knew they were Jewish. Tullio had questioned him about his religion, but it was the subject of Marxism that really set them off. Alessandro elaborated on Professor Brenda's words, while Tullio reworked those of the "reds" in his dormitory.

Persecution of the Jews? Tullio grew impassioned. It wouldn't have made any sense in the great socialist brotherhood, as long as Moses' descendants stopped claiming their own traditions. Otherwise, what would happen to the idea of equality among all people?

Alessandro agreed in principle, but he was troubled and argumentative with him. Against his own will, the rabbi's little speech about the leaf falling off the tree and losing its identity kept coming to mind. What about Alma? Without the persecution, he wouldn't have changed schools and they would never have gotten to know one another. How stupid could he be? The last thing he needed was a rogue thought like that to torment him. He would meet someone else, of course. But does that mean love isn't an absolute choice, either? If we're so influenced by what goes on in the outside world, how can we find ourselves? He knew he wasn't a good Jew, but now he was racked by the doubt that he wasn't a good Communist either.

Tullio had found out about his one-day affair with the soldier's wife and teased him about it. "You'll see. The war will come to an end, the soldier will be back, and he'll stick a knife into you," he said laughing. Alessandro laughed with him, but he couldn't stop thinking that if the war came to an end, his father would no longer be an enemy of the state. He didn't want to raise his hopes too much, though.

News travelled fast. "Turn the radio on! Italy has asked for an armistice!" After the breaking news at eight that evening, Marshal Badoglio's proclamation recorded for Italian state radio was broadcast every half hour. Alessandro and his parents listened to the speech over and over again. Sergeant Capriotti was there beside them, even though it wasn't Radio London they were listening to.

"The Italian government, recognizing the impossibility of continuing the unequal struggle against an overwhelming enemy force, in order to avoid further and graver disasters for the Nation, has sought an armistice from General Eisenhower [. . .]. The request was granted." Marc waited for the closing words: "Consequently, all acts of hostility against the Anglo-American forces by Italian forces must cease everywhere."

All acts of hostility . . . must cease . . . . must cease . . . everywhere. Even in the boondocks where an ordinary British citizen, named Marc Rimon, was being held prisoner.

Marc looked at the sergeant in trepidation but found no trace of the warmth he had shown the evening the Fascist regime fell. He limited himself to shaking his hand, almost formally. He was thinking of the Germans who had taken up residence in the army barracks just outside town. Rumor had it that there were a few SS units in their midst. He didn't want the Rimons to find out.

The town bells started to ring. People thronged into the streets, shouting and cheering with joy. A mother or two started making up beds, preparing for their sons' imminent return.

After a desperate resistance at the San Paolo gate, Rome

capitulates to the Germans. The King with his entire family, the government in office, and the entire High Command flee the capital at dawn and head south. The Italian Army is disbanded just as German troops are garrisoned all over the country. Then the Americans land in Salerno. People are dumbfounded. They don't know which way to look, who to turn to, what to do, or who the enemy is.

Sergeant Capriotti rushed in at an unusual hour compared to his regular evening visits. He didn't even sit down. He grabbed Marc by the arm and said "Go, go now! You need to get out of here as soon as possible."

"Are we . . . are we free?" Marc stammered, bewildered.

"You're not free; you're in danger. I don't know who will give me my next orders or what they will be. I'm telling you to leave in secret, on my own initiative. Is that clear?"

"Yes, but where?" Marc was too shocked to think straight.

"I don't know," Capriotti all but yelled. "You're not being moved with an official ordinance in your hand, don't you get it?" For years, Marc had gotten used to moving only where the official documents had erected walls around him. The sergeant slowly understood what his problem was and calmed down a little. "Go back home, to Genoa, and decide when you're there. You have friends, right? Get them to help you, advise you, or whatever," he said softly.

Alessandro wasn't there. He was out with Tullio. His father waited anxiously for him to come back, which was two hours later. They told him what had happened.

"I'm not coming. I'm not going back home with you." Alessandro was completely calm. He told them that he and Tullio had decided to go up into the mountains and join the partisans there.

"You're just two kids. Who would take you into battle?" Emilia whispered, scornfully, a shadow of concern darkening her face nonetheless. Marc tried to reason with his son at length. "This time, I'm not letting anyone humiliate me," Alessandro said. His father wasn't against his plan; he was just pointing out that nobody had ever seen a partisan up there in the boondocks.

Tullio and Alessandro left at dawn the following day. Marc tried to assuage his anxiety. Tullio's father was the family doctor for the whole valley. He would be sure to receive news of his son and his son's friend one way or another.

Emilia had started packing slowly.

Alessandro was tall for his age, but his face was as fresh, smooth, and round as a boy's. Tullio was small and skinny. His thick glasses lent him a maturity beyond his years. He looked more like a seminarist from his school in Piedmont than a warrior.

And indeed nobody takes them for warriors; vagabonds, maybe, as layers of dust begin to coat them. People are suspicious and shut the door on them when they knock asking for news, mumbling the word "partisans." They are too young to be demobbed soldiers, not one old peasant woman gives them a piece of bread. As they roam across the fields, there is nothing left to pick on the sly to satisfy their hunger. They climb mountains and find forgotten villages, but there is not a trace of the partisans.

The prior of an old monastery at the top of a bare hill saves them from starvation. After feeding them bowl after bowl of vegetable soup, he starts castigating them as if he were the head teacher at their school. Tullio, for some reason, feels obliged to reveal his name, his father's profession, and everything else. "Go back to school and study. That is the only way you will be really useful to our country," the prior says severely. He turns to Alessandro, adding, "You too," with a little more benevolence.

They get back home at sunset, famished and filthy after

three days wandering around the countryside. Marc is still tying string around the boxes of possessions that don't fit into the suitcases. When he sees his son, he stops, the ball of string mid-air. Alessandro shrugs. "We couldn't find the partisans," he says. His father answers, "We're leaving tomorrow."

Alessandro thinks that as soon as he gets to Genoa, he must go and visit Professor Brenda.

CHAPTER 36

T he professor is not here, he's gone away." The concierge spoke hastily, looking furtively around her, as if some disaster or other were looming from the other side of the courtyard. "Will he be back when school starts?" She didn't know. He had left her his cat to look after, a cantankerous mog it was, too.

Alessandro dragged his feet all the way home.

Nonno Luigi had not yet returned to the house. He had had a bad cough and a little fever, and Aunt Wanda didn't want to tire him unnecessarily with the move. Luigi complained, "I want to go home." Wanda was offended because "home" was Emilia's house, and Emilia had certainly never treated him as well as she did.

Marc was restless now he was home. He had been away three years; his old workbench looked worn-out and strange. The place where they had lived for a lifetime was no longer a safe harbor; they were only there because they didn't know where else to go. Any day now, somebody could knock at the door and arrest him again. Because he was Jewish, perhaps. Outside these walls nothing was sure. Mussolini had been freed by paratroopers flown in from Germany, and a Fascist republic had been set up in Salò. Squads of German troops combed the streets looking for young Italian men who had escaped from the army to enroll them by force.

"Don't wear long pants," his mother pleaded. She wet his hair and combed it with a side parting to make him look like a child. Alessandro let her do it. Since going to Professor Brenda's house and not finding him, he had been in a trance. It was as if he had lost the will to fight.

One day it happened. The Germans stopped a tram, blocked all the doors, and checked the passengers one by one. They took one look at him and let him get off with the women and the older men. He watched them march away, digging the tips of their rifles into the backs of three young men in civvies. One of them, wearing a striped tie and a hat, waved "*ciao*" with his hand. He looked like Uncle Osvaldo, only younger.

The Jews in the city thrashed out the matter, amidst waves of anxiety and ripples of optimism. The Jewish population in Italy was quite small; there would be no point in waging a campaign against them. In any case, the rabbi had hidden the register of names and addresses of the Jews who had enrolled in the community in a safe place. How would the authorities ever find the Jews without any information? Moreover, many of them had left, and could not be gotten hold of. "What do they care about ordinary folk like us?" Emilia fretted, turning to her husband with a worried, almost suspicious, look in her eye. Why did he never deign to answer her?

One morning, not long after dawn, they heard someone knocking insistently on the door. One arm leaning on the doorpost, a beret pulled down over his eyes, and his usual, unshakeable smile—there was the unexpected figure of Lelio, the great man who had saved so many Viennese Jews. Throwing himself onto a chair inside, and speaking agitatedly, he told them that the organization had been disbanded with the Germans occupying the country, but then a miracle had taken place. The Archdiocese of Vienna had been happy to continue their work. The Cardinal in person, with a fearless young assistant, had set up a close network of parish priests, monks, and nuns who were working at full throttle.

Lelio spoke animatedly, driven by an urge to describe the people he'd encountered, adding episodes and minute details of their lives as he did so. But then, he suddenly stopped in his tracks, like a sprinter digging in his heels and swaying side to side before coming to a halt. "I didn't come to take stock of our organizational problems," he muttered. "I came to talk about you. What are you doing still in this house?" He shouted so unexpectedly that even Marc flinched. "Are you really convinced that the Germans have no intention of getting the Italian Jews? Did you know that the few remaining Jews in Merano have been deported already?"

They had no idea. They were struck dumb by the news. Their friend lowered his voice again. They were not in the category of the neediest, as they had money and family, and they were allowed to move freely around the city; they should get their act together and clear out quick. "Oh, and let the rest of your family know," was his final word of advice.

"Being optimistic at any cost can be stupid," he said, with a big smile, on his way out. It may have been his way of making it up to them, after his fit of anger before.

The next time the doorbell rang it was the concierge. Next to her stood a plump old woman, who was gasping for breath after climbing the stairs. She looked working-class, and clearly not accustomed to elevators. The reason why their concierge had felt the need to come with her soon became clear. It was to do with their jobs: the old woman, too, was a concierge. "Don't you remember?" she asked, looking at Emilia. "I was the porter at your parents' house. When you were a little girl, there was another woman, but then I came along and you met me."

Yes, come to think of it, Emilia did remember her, but she didn't dare enquire why she'd come all the way up the stairs to see her.

"Two policemen came," she told them. "Two men with rifles, and they were looking for your mother. They had a sheet in their hands with her name on it."

"My mother? But she died more than fifteen years ago!" Emilia had turned pale, and her husband had to hold her up.

"I know. That's why I came to tell you."

Were they policemen or soldiers? Italians or Germans? Marc desperately tried to find out more. The old woman grew confused but insisted they had been carrying rifles. That was why she'd been scared of them. She told them that she'd remembered she had the Rimons' address. She'd tucked it away, because after the mourning period was over, she'd started sending on their mail. That was why she'd thought it better to come over straight away and tell them in person, wasn't that the right thing to do?

"How's old Luigi?" she asked, but she lowered her voice as a sign of respect in case he had passed away.

"He doesn't live with us right now, he's in hospital," Emilia answered hastily. Marc looked sideways at her. Whatever his wife was thinking, it worried him.

"In hospital? Why did you say 'in hospital' of all places?" They'd never seen Osvaldo so upset. She had simply said the first thing that had come into her head to put the woman off her trail, Emilia answered hesitantly. She was so shocked that she didn't over-react to the criticism as she would usually have done. "She thought the old concierge had come to spy on us," Marc tried to defend his wife. "But it doesn't make sense. Who would go to all that trouble to look for two old people like that, one of whom is dead?" He kept his eye on his brother-in-law as he spoke. Why was he so worked up?

"Hospital," Osvaldo went on repeating as he sank into an armchair. "I've been working for days to get my old father-in-law to the safety of a hospital," he murmured under his breath.

"It was top secret, and madam here already knows every-thing."

"I made it up! I just told you!" Emilia said, leaping out of her seat, but there was no vehemence in her tone. The good old days when fighting and having arguments was permissible were over. She noticed that her sister was quietly crying over in the corner, and Alessandro was standing there, mute and immobile, listening to them.

They knew Luigi was ill. He was refusing to get out of bed these days, though he might also have been making a point. Dr. Marcenaro had said the old man had widespread inflammation of the respiratory system, a condition that was a little worse than pneumonia. There was nothing more urgent than taking care of him now. "I'd managed," Osvaldo explained, gaining a little verve as he spoke. He'd met a doctor who was a member of the Resistance who was willing to keep Luigi in his ward for as long as necessary. He couldn't be registered with a Jewish last name, but Osvaldo had solved that problem, too. Old Giovanna, who had kept house for them for years and was now retired, had agreed to pretend Luigi was an uncle who'd come up from the South to get treatment. She had also agreed to go and visit him regularly in the hospital. They had procured fake papers for him using her own last name. Osvaldo couldn't resist adding a little detail to the story even in that moment of tension. Her last name was Di Luigi. A great coincidence, right? He would always answer to the name, however confused he might be between his first name and his last!

"Will we be able to go and see him, too?" Alessandro asked directly. His uncle's final quip had disturbed him. It was offen-sive, he felt, to the dignity of suffering.

Osvaldo grabbed him by the shoulders and gave him an affectionate squeeze. "No, Alessandro. This is exactly what we have been called upon to renounce. None of us must be seen there. We might be recognized, and, if we are, the whole house of cards will collapse." He would stay in touch with Giovanna regularly, and that would be it. Silence fell in the room. "Can I go and say goodbye to him now?" Alessandro asked.

"They're sending me to hospital, you know." his grandfather joked, sarcastically.

Alessandro nodded. "That way you can kill two birds with one stone. You can get better and hide from danger," he said, feeling his tone was insincere.

"I'll get better, I'll get better," he said, shaking his head rhythmically, as if there were music inside his it.

"Come on! You've always said, "Better a living dog than a dead lion."

"No, I'd rather be the lion."

Alessandro knew what he meant.

CHAPTER 37

"Where's your grandmother? Where is she?" The German was shaking him, twisting his arm forcefully. He was strangely young, almost like a child. Now it was Hermann shaking him, a blood-red wound on his forehead. So, he hadn't left after all? Why was he asking him with that sneer on his face where his grandmother was?

Alessandro woke up dripping with sweat, his arm aching. He slept fitfully these days. Every time a truck drove by, he jumped out of his skin and his heart thumped on and on, even when the rumble of engines had vanished into the night.

"When are we leaving?" he kept asking his father, who always answered, "We need to get organized." Osvaldo was frantically organizing Nonno Luigi's move to the hospital. He was running from one side of the city to the other and was never home. "We'd better wait until we can talk to him," he said one evening, looking sideways at his son and speaking like an ill-prepared student.

"Why?" Alessandro yelled. "Why do we need them? Can't we organize things ourselves?"

"We're family. It's normal to consult one another, especially at times like these," Emilia butted in. When her son didn't answer, she added, "Yes, we now know about the deportation of the Jews in Merano, but as far as the rest of Italy is concerned . . . The Germans have been here for over a month, and nothing has happened yet. There's the Vatican here in Italy; they won't dare do anything extreme."

Her son looked daggers at her. She stepped back, intimidated, feeling like she was losing the battle.

Why his wife could never abstain from criticizing her son, whatever he did or said, was a mystery to Marc. His behavior might sometimes seem a little smug, but there was something heroic about it, yet she always had to turn up the corners of her mouth in a scornful grimace. And now? Now that the boy was laying bare his weakness, offering it to her as a gift, there she was, subjugated by her son, looking at him with ingratiating condescension.

Marc didn't get it. Emilia was not aware of it either, but she had instinctively grasped the message that nature defends itself. She had seen the primordial energy of a creature that wants to survive at all cost, and she had lowered her head out of respect. Her son's terror was the awakening of a warrior.

Finally, Osvaldo called. "We'll set off soon. They're waiting for us," Marc informed his wife. Emilia turned imperceptibly towards her son, as if she wanted to check whether he was ready.

When they met Osvaldo, he was restless and worn out. Moving Luigi to the hospital had been fraught with endless practical and psychological problems. "He asked me to say goodbye to the child. I think he meant you many years ago," he told Alessandro flatly, shaking his head. Luigi had begun ranting and raving so often; he was no longer himself. All these changes must have unhinged his already fragile state of mind. Wanda had made things even more difficult. She had cried the whole time and every now and again threatened to go and visit her father in the hospital—"Just once," she pleaded. Osvaldo had had to compromise and take her to the doctor's private surgery, so that he could update her on the latest developments of his illness. The doctor had vaguely reassured her regarding the old man's health, but, as a member of the Resistance, he had returned to his main point. "The Germans will not spare the Jews in this city, that's for sure," he had said. "Clear out of the house as soon as you can and do not show up at the places you normally do," he'd advised them over and over.

Wanda had fallen into a state of despair again. She was sitting there, her hair disheveled, lost in thought. She hadn't even bothered to put her pearl necklace on. Every now and then, she shot a reproachful glance at her sister. Emilia hadn't asked once about her father; who was she was keeping her tears for?

Osvaldo explained in a low voice that the high-quality false papers being prepared for them would be there any day now. As with Nonno Luigi, they would be registered as citizens from the South escaping the Allied Armies. The front had split Italy in two, so nobody could actually check their details in the local administrative offices. Once they had new identities, they planned to move to the suburbs where nobody would recognize them and move again if it became necessary.

His speech was over. What else could he say? The circumstances would shape their plans for the future. Osvaldo roused himself and looked at his brother-in-law. "You need to go, too," he said urgently, as if it had suddenly become clear to him. Marc was in double jeopardy as an enemy alien. "Get yourselves papers as soon as possible and make a plan." He grew agitated as he spoke, perhaps to cover his embarrassment.

Silence filled the room. Alessandro stared at his mother and father. They looked petrified. Then Marc responded: "Of course. I'm sure we'll manage."

Before leaving, his aunt rushed to Alessandro's side and drew him into a hug. "Whatever you do, stay safe!" she cried, tears running down her face.

That was the day Alessandro said goodbye to his almost second mother.

"I'm two years older than him," Marc said through his teeth after they'd walked a good stretch of the road in silence.

"Than who?" Emilia asked, desperately pretending not to understand.

"He's not the patriarch of the family. It's not his duty to take care of us. He's already done more than enough." By the time Marc presented his second round of thoughts they were already sitting at the table. Nobody touched their food.

"He's left us on our own! He knows everybody, and we don't know anyone!" Emilia exploded.

It wasn't true: Osvaldo had always done everything in his power to help them in emergencies, and he'd bust his gut to get his father-in-law sorted out. Marc tried to persuade his wife to be reasonable. "And now he's got to take care of your fragile wisp of a sister," he said pensively.

"Fragile wisp" is what their father had called Wanda, and Alessandro was overtaken by a sense of pity for his aunt, who was terrified, and yet all she could think about was leaving behind her beloved nephew.

"A whole group can't seek refuge together. We must each look after ourselves." We're still young enough to be able to plan things on our own. Marc scrutinized his son.

Alessandro answered, "In the meantime, let's get out of this house."

He shadowed his father, who had gone into his workshop and was dubiously leafing through his client address book. "I'm trying to behave like your uncle," he said, with a bitter smile. "I used to have quite a few rich clients who were very fond of me, but now . . . I don't know . . ." Does being rich necessarily mean you have connections with power? Perhaps. There was that couple that had come to see him in hospital. They owned a chain of hotels on the coast. Who knows? This was all just pondering and wondering; there was no substance

to it. The big brown address book ended up thrown onto the
worktop with a theatrical gesture.

A crumpled scrap of paper fell out of the book at that precise moment. In capital letters, written in pen, was the name
"FAUSTO" with a Milan address and phone number followed
by an address and number in Genoa. He chose the Genoa one,
hoping fate would be kinder to them.

"The Martelli household," a male voice answered promptly.
It was Fausto; Marc recognized his voice immediately.

"It's Marc. You know you offered to help me a long time
ago . . . ?" he ventured hesitantly.

"Do you still live at the same address? Stay there. I'll be
with you within the hour," was the precipitous answer, as if
someone had been standing by the phone the whole time waiting for his call.

At least seven years must have gone by, perhaps more, but
Marc had a clear image of the young man, who had been cast
out by his entire family and who had one day asked to speak to
him, saying honestly, "I've come to you because you're foreign."

With the same tousled hair as when he was younger, Fausto
listened carefully and asked continuous questions. "I'll be back
soon," he said hastily. Two hours later, he was indeed back.
Jole had been quite upset to hear that someone had gone to
look up a Jewish woman who had died several years before at
her old address. It must mean there are lists, Fausto explained.
He dropped the name "Jole" into the conversation as if it were
totally normal.

"Pack your bags," he urged them, with a new confidence in
his voice. "I'll come and pick you up tomorrow." He told them
that he and Jole had decided to put them up at their house
until they could hatch a failsafe escape plan. Leaving the house
right away was, according to Jole, imperative.

CHAPTER 38

A great deal of time had gone by—he had been just a kid at the time, traipsing around with his mother on an errand to a seamstress in the suburbs—but the image of that beautiful brunette had stayed with him ever since. He even remembered the sideways glance she had given them, almost as if she was torn between wanting and not wanting to meet them. The clash of the two desires was intoxicating. He had thought about it a lot since then: it was one of those things about life that he still needed to figure out.

And now there she was. She had welcomed them into her home, a little apartment in an upper story of a building. Light streamed in from all sides, and the peacock design on the wallpaper had faded. Jole, however, hadn't faded; she was just the same as back then. She looked at them, and it was clear that she expected admiration from the two men and hostility from the woman. You could also see that she was confident that the woman would soon capitulate too. Mother Nature's nourishment is there for everyone, and everyone takes what they can. It was evident at skin level that this young woman possessed a sensuality that did not shine its light on anything specific; it ranged around her in a wide, sweeping beam, its rays making every aspect of her life, every single thing she did, shimmer.

She started taking care of their needs without any preamble, without any need for a smile, even. There was no need for words, either; they were expressed in her actions. She bustled around them like someone who, out of a long-held habit, makes bread every day for the family.

The most important thing was getting hold of false papers. Without new identities there was no way they could plan the first step. They were to stay in the apartment at all times; they'd had no idea how much danger they'd been in back home. In an impersonal tone—it was a practical matter, after all—Jole started interrogating them about the family's finances. High-quality counterfeit travel papers had a hefty price tag, and what they were planning for the following leg of the journey was even more expensive. The idea was to escape to Switzerland. It had been decided that leaving Italy was the best plan, given that Marc had a foreign passport. The organization that would smuggle them across the border had already been contacted, but they, too, demanded a tidy sum.

While his partner spoke, Fausto looked around the room. He was both embarrassed and anxious, but there was no need to be either since Marc was answering all her questions with the collaborative zeal of a new convert. Jole's expression had also lit up: the Rimon family savings were sufficient to save their lives, and there may even be a little something left over for "after."

"You put yourself entirely at her mercy. You've told her all our private business," Emilia complained that evening in their room. Marc said, "We were already at her mercy." He had noticed that their hostess was buying most of their food on the black market as she couldn't use the ration cards in their name without putting them at risk. He had asked her awkwardly whether they could contribute in any way to the expense, but she had just waved him away with her hand.

"Where does she go? Why is she always going out?" Emilia fretted whenever she saw young Jole leave the house dressed to the nines in vertiginous heels as if there were no war on at all. Marc shrugged absently.

"Aren't you planning on getting out yourselves?" Marc asked Fausto one day when they were alone.

"No, I'm as safe I can be here. Didn't you notice that I call myself Martelli, using her name?" Fausto explained. Jole helped many people, but she wasn't one of those profiteers that pop up when the occasion demands it. She knew people in high places, people who couldn't easily be labeled as belonging to one side or another. Wars come to an end sooner or later, and her name was highly respected in many circles of society.

"Now she is taking care of you. You're the first members of my family to set foot in this house." Fausto looked gratified, fulfilled even, like somebody dying of hunger who finally gets a good meal. He went on to tell Marc, in such a rush of words that he was almost incomprehensible, that he had arranged for his parents to stay in a convent up in the Piedmont Alps. They had had to implement the plan through an intermediary, while his parents had pretended not to realize that their son must have been behind the whole thing.

"You welcomed me into your home when all my family, *all* of them, had slammed the door in my face." Marc felt a stab of shame. He remembered feeling pressured into meeting him, or lacking the resolve to deny him. Or maybe not.

The papers were ready and had been paid for. Their new name was Ferrari. In his new identity, Marc—who was born in the Belgian city of Antwerp, Anversa in Italian—had been assigned a birthplace that by a trick of destiny sounded almost identical: the town of Aversa, in the southern region of Campania. His wife and son would share the last name and address.

The papers and ration cards, with all the right duty stamps on them, were perfect. They were not counterfeit; they had almost certainly been produced by a complicit administrative office. Alessandro busied himself roughing them up in his hands; he had been given the job of making them look used. He realized Jole was watching him, and she smiled at him for the first time.

The movement had come to put their escape plan into action.

"First, you will take a train to Milan. There will be somebody waiting for you there." Fausto took over the explanation. He felt it necessary to describe everything in great detail, and he knew Jole wouldn't have bothered. The most important thing was to find a reliable and expert smuggler to get them over the Swiss border. They would have to wait for however long it took, possibly days. Milan was where they would wait. They would be staying in the apartment of a man called Giovanni. At this point Fausto faltered, as if painfully turning over the words in his hands. Old Giovanni had always loved Jole. He called her his "little *tüseta*," and, as his oldest friend when her father had died, he had practically adopted her.

There was no need for them to know exactly who Giovanni was. He was a boss, and if there were people in his circles who were involved in organized crime, it didn't really need to be mentioned. The thing that was, however, worth highlighting was the fact that he was willing to accommodate these "new relatives" in his house. This was why Fausto had wanted to be the one doing the explaining.

Luggage. Just what was essential; they would take good care of their belongings here, together with their old papers—their real identities—which would be indispensable once the war was over. Marc's British passport would be handed over to the Swiss Legation, which had overseen British interests in the city since war had been declared.

Jole took over next, speaking in a detached tone of voice, with a deadpan expression.

"He has to look as young as he can. Two adults and a child is the ideal for crossing the border and being accepted in

Switzerland." Jole fixed her eyes on Alessandro and Emilia while she spoke.

"I'm sixteen. How can I look like a child?" Alessandro was growing nervous. "Younger" and "more childish" were the words that had accompanied him at every stage of his life, even though the context was different now. It was now his destiny to be a "child."

Short pants? No, his legs had become more muscular recently. Rather, plus-fours and knee-high socks, Jole and Emilia agreed while Alessandro's mind wandered elsewhere.

"Leave something from your childhood in the suitcase. I bet you brought some comic books, trading cards, or something like that, right?" Jole asked him. Yes, he had a collection of trading cards of the famous cyclists in the Giro d'Italia with him, as well as some marbles and two issues of *L'avventuroso*. As he rummaged in his cloth bag, a marble rolled out. He pulled out the cardboard box Nonno Luigi had made for him.

Alessandro held the gold chain with the Star of David pendant in his hands.

"It goes without saying that you can't take that, right?" Jole whispered, looking him straight in the eye.

"Of course I'm taking it with me; I've never been separated from it in my life." Alessandro stared back at Jole with a look that was too calm to be challenging.

They had run away from home, gotten themselves false papers, and paid for them using up most of the family savings, they were about to travel across a part of the country that was infested with Germans, and this boy, who had triggered the whole thing with his panic, was now jeopardizing everything with an incomprehensible provocation, prepared to put their lives at risk by stubbornly insisting on bringing with him—maybe even wearing, around his neck, why not?—a symbol that the Germans and Fascists had appropriated to brand Jews as infamous! Never in his life had Marc been so bowled over by his son.

"I know all the things that you are saying, but I also know I have to bring it with me." Alessandro continued to look at the others with a steady, almost placid, gaze. He didn't say anything more. Nobody else said anything either. They realized that this was not a whim.

Emilia looked at her son. There were times at synagogue that she couldn't find the translation of a prayer they were chanting in the *tefillah*. In the end, just listening, without understanding the words, made her spirit soar. She didn't know why, but it made her feel a rush of something like humility, reverence towards the mystery of life and the people that lived on this earth. This felt almost the same. Emilia was overwhelmed by the force of a message that could not be grasped through normal channels.

"Hand me your jacket," she said slowly to her son. Then she asked Jole if she could borrow her sewing box. With everyone watching, she starting unpicking the seams of the jacket at the top of the sleeve, slipped the chain inside, and sewed everything back up again with tiny, almost invisible stitches.

CHAPTER 39

Getting arrested because you can't find your way to an address would be the most ill-considered thing ever. That is exactly what would have happened if they had carried on wandering around Milan clutching their bags in an area that was miles from the station. Black-market runners or suspicious escapees—little imagination was needed as to why they might find themselves locked in a prison cell.

The train journey had gone well. The ticket inspector, flanked by a soldier, had asked for their papers. He'd looked at them distractedly and gone on to the next passenger.

Emilia decided to ask for directions. She opted for a fruit-seller who immediately started gesticulating and speaking in dialect. Emilia was scared. She didn't want to appear foreign, so she answered in Genoese dialect, which she thought might be similar since she had understood almost everything. The woman looked a little puzzled and then carried on with her directions, shouting a little louder this time. They found their way. Via Confalonieri, number 9 was a gray building of just two floors. The front door looked as though it had just been repainted, but there had clearly been a lack of paint available and each section was a different shade of green.

The man who opened the door to them was as big and solid as a mountain. His deeply wrinkled face was given character by his bright blue eyes that looked straight into you from the first moment. There was no need for introductions. "He looks like Venanzio," Alessandro commented when they were alone. His father didn't agree. "Venanzio's features are more regular." As well as his bulky stature, Giovanni was endowed with a nose of remarkable proportions that reigned over his whole face. "For a man who is that ugly, he is really quite handsome," Emilia thought, but kept it to herself.

Giovanni's wife, whose hair had been permed so badly it looked scorched, was called Carletta—or, at least, that was what her husband called her affectionately. She was petite, good-natured, and bustled around the house. She was the one that led them to their room, where a rollaway bed had been pulled out next to the double. Bang in the middle, under a crucifix nailed to the wall, there was a doll in a sky-blue dress with folds and folds of white frills giving volume to her skirt.

The doll stared at them mutely, but the rest of the house was by no means silent. They could hear the pitter-patter of hurried steps through the ceiling and of furniture being dragged about. They had seen the stairwell but knew there couldn't be any family members. Jole had told them that Giovanni didn't have any kids, and that was why he'd taken such a shine to her. So, they must be guests. Guests like them? Fellow escapees, perhaps? Were there many people being handled by the smugglers? Marc glanced at his son and saw that Alessandro was as nervous as he was.

Giovanni summoned Marc and led him in silence to a room at the end of the corridor that must have been his private office. Emilia and Alessandro followed them mechanically. The "boss" turned to Alessandro and said, "You look bright enough, you can listen, too."

Emilia was left standing in the corridor on her own and felt duty-bound to go and see where Carletta with her scorched hair-do was.

"You'd better believe it when I tell you that getting into Switzerland is not easy these days." Giovanni dove right in to the subject, without a moment's hesitation. "If only you'd thought of it earlier!" he sighed, stretching out on his chair. After the armistice on September 8, the border had been unguarded for more than a week. There were no checkpoints; anyone could get in. The ability to take advantage of the right moment is an art so few people have mastered. Thousands had managed, though: Italian soldiers who had deserted in order not to serve under the Germans, clutches of partisans in dire danger, Jews and other categories at risk. They had all made it. "It only lasted a few days. Now the border is guarded by the Swiss and the Germans." Giovanni was losing his thread as he elaborated on his own story.

"Okay!" he said, thumping his fist on the table in a friendly fashion, as if he were stamping the sealing wax on a contract. "You're here because you need to cross the Swiss border. And we will get you across." Relying on the smugglers was fraught with danger, there was no point in denying it. By now, both the cities and the mountain passes were infested with improvised criminals, imposters who charged obscene amounts of money and then abandoned their charges half-way up the mountain or, worse, informed on them to the Germans and cashed in on the bounty. Some had even created a false border with stakes and rolls of barbed wire; they would convince the escapees they were safely over the frontier and then calmly walk away.

"That's why my little *tüseta* sent you to me. And she did the right thing. We're practically family, aren't we?" For the first time, Giovanni smiled, winking at Alessandro. It was true, Jole had bewitched him: he spied on her from the corridor and hated it when she went out all dressed up. But how did *he* know about that? Alessandro squirmed at the thought.

"There's one more thing I need to explain," Giovanni said,

yanking his "almost relative" by the arm as he stood up to leave. There were other people in the building; he'd heard them, right? They're friends, nothing more. They sometimes met to discuss things. "All they know about you is that you're Fausto's cousin, but tonight you'd better join us. There's someone you need to meet." Then, looking Marc straight in the eye, he said, "I'm sure you know what to say and what not to say." Looking at Alessandro, he added lightly, "You don't need to come. You're a kid and you'll get bored."

They sat around a table and took turns to speak after raising their hands, as if they were in a board meeting.

"What do you do?" a skinny little man, who until then had been talking about safes, asked Marc. "Diamonds." The answer slipped out effortlessly. Marc felt a warm rush of satisfaction for having been able to lie without actually lying. He could see that he had triggered the interest of the others and was surprised to find that he was describing his craft to them with unnecessary enthusiasm. The most fashionable cut nowadays? The "emerald cut," of course, but nobody wanted anything frivolous anymore. There was tragedy looming, and mostly people came to him to extract gems from rings and necklaces, since they sold better unmounted. What was left of their beloved jewelry was dumped in a hurry as if it were scrap metal. But of course, there was a niche market there, too, with opportunistic dealers rapaciously swooping in for the kill. The laws and regulations were no longer upheld; everybody wanted to take advantage of everyone else. "It's the time for assassins," Marc said under his breath.

A deafening silence fell. A lanky blond with a protruding forehead, who was younger than the others, stared at him. "It's him." The thought flashed into Marc's head. "Our life depends on this man." They all started talking again, their speech weaving together. Every now and again, one or another turned to Marc, as if they were seeking his agreement.

"Are they all thieves?" Emilia asked fearfully that evening when they were in bed.

"Do you prefer exterminators?" Marc was almost smiling. Nobody would understand, but he felt at peace. He had been part of a group of human beings who had listened to what he had been saying happily, as if he were one of them. It was the first time in years and years. He'd rather be in a band of thieves than cast out, *out* of everything.

The next morning, he was called to Giovanni's study again. On one side of the desk sat the blond guy with the sticking-out forehead. Marc's instinct had been correct: he was, indeed, their smuggler.

There was no preamble this time, either. His name was Saverio. His father, an old friend of Giovanni's, was the best-known and most glorious smuggler in the area, long before the war. These were the only personal details Giovanni was prepared to give while imparting his hastily delivered instructions.

As he spoke, he laid a massive hand on Saverio's shoulder, a gesture which the young man put up with, but he didn't bother hiding his irritation. He clearly didn't appreciate his father being mentioned, although the old man thought he was doing him a favor.

"It's best to agree on everything before we go into any detail," the blond man said impassively. He knew the papers had been paid for and that his task was to negotiate the family's passage to Switzerland.

"Twenty-five thousand," Giovanni whispered.

The blond lowered his eyes. "Too little for three people."

"It's what they can pay. Don't we want to leave them some margin for when they get there?"

"As it's you asking me. They're your relatives . . ." Marc was feeling uneasy, as if the guy was being sarcastic when he said they were family. Maybe it was just fear giving him ideas. "We guarantee you get over the border. Once you're in Switzerland, you're on your own." Now that Saverio had taken the lead again, he had no intention of letting anyone else speak for him. It wasn't a great moment for hospitality; they were refusing hundreds of people these days. "They choose who to save and who to send back. In the end, the last word lies with the border guards." The young man had said too much and was already regretting it. Why scare his "clients"? What he wanted was for them to appreciate that he was not simply a runner; he knew everything there was to know every step of the way. How stupid, he thought. They probably knew it all, too. "We'll get you to the other side," he repeated. "And believe me, with all the scum up there getting in our way, that's already a lot. He would tell them what day and what time they'd be leaving soon. He had evidently finished his set piece.

Twenty-five thousand more! The savings of a lifetime were slipping through their fingers in a matter of days. In their room with the rest of the family, Marc was more shocked than worried. "They're called savings because you set them aside for times like these," Alessandro said harshly. He then asked more hesitantly, "How much do you have left?"

"More or less the same figure I've just given them." Would it be enough to live on for a potentially long period in Switzerland? Marc started torturing himself again. Emilia didn't say a word. The doll in the frilly skirt, now sitting on top of the wardrobe, continued to stare at her, a stunned expression in her eyes.

They stood around the table. The blond guy arrived very late and whispered something into Giovanni's ear. "Tomorrow morning," the "boss" said to Marc. He had already guessed. He had handed over the envelope with the money inside a while back.

"The first leg will be by train to Como." This was the only information he gave. "The mountains begin there. Dress warmly, it's cold up there."

Giovanni looked at them as if he were already missing them.

CHAPTER 40

Here they are, ready, a little before dawn, standing by the door with their suitcases in their hands. The blond smuggler is wearing a baggy jacket and a dark-gray woolen hat pulled right down over his forehead. He looks at the boy. "Where's your hat?" he demands.

"Son, don't you know that it's cold in Milan in October but up in the mountains, it's even colder?" Giovanni's voice over rides young Saverio's.

Alessandro pulls a heavy woolen cap with a visor out of his bag and sticks it on his head nervously. Giovanni is wearing a coat and hat, too. They all look at him; they don't understand. Is he planning on coming with them to the station? When the train arrives, he gets on with them. Saverio looks unhappy; offended, almost. After the first stop, Saverio breaks down and asks, "Why are you coming with us?"

"They're family, okay?" Giovanni answers, with a twinkle in his eye.

The blond guy locks himself into a sullen silence. Alessandro knows why, and he's on the younger man's side, but Giovanni's presence is certainly a great comfort.

During the journey, their tickets and papers are checked. This time, too, as on the trip from Genoa to Milan, everything seems to trundle along as peacefully as the gentle rocking of the train.

Their welcome in the station is a prelude. Running boot heels echoing, strangled voices giving one another the chase, barked orders, and then a shot. Two German soldiers drag the inert body of a young man dripping with blood. The five travelers who have just gotten off the train are in their path. The young man stares at them and manages to yell "Help!" before the soldiers jerk him away. The five stand there, gawping at the scene, before shuffling off. "This is the way Como greets us," Emilia muttered, her lips deadly pale.

"Take your food stamps out, we're going to a restaurant." These are Saverio's scant instructions. The dining room is small—more like a tavern than a restaurant—but the walls are lined with light-colored wood, and the fire in the hearth is lit. A few tables are occupied by German soldiers in uniform. Alessandro stops in his tracks, paralyzed. Saverio orders him to sit down and chat with his father or anyone else he chooses. He, meanwhile, is nodding hello to one person after another, people of all ages. He seems to know many of them, and exchanges pleasantries with a few. The tavern keeper plants a hand on his shoulder and whispers something in his ear. Saverio laughs as if he's just heard the funniest of jokes.

Alessandro is attempting to talk to Giovanni, but he is unable to eat. Every now and again, he puts something in his mouth and sends it down with a gulp of water as he would if he were swallowing some disgusting medicine. It's nearly the end of their lunch when their "guide" fills them in on the next leg of the journey. His tone is now that of someone who has never joked or played around in his life. They will soon be climbing Mt. Bisbino. So late? Will they be crossing the border at night? Marc asks quietly. No, they'll take a break up on the mountain and the crossing will be at dawn.

Saverio gets up and the others stand, too. Dazed, they start pulling their bags out from under the table. Giovanni stays sitting. "Shall we go?" Saverio asks him sharply. Giovanni doesn't answer. He waves his hand to say no and grumbles, "I have to catch the train back to Milan."

Giovanni is glued to the table. That's what he's decided. It might be wisdom, it might be age.

They grow quieter and quieter as they climb higher. The silence of the mountain is majestic and eternal, whereas theirs is the silence of insignificant beings dragging out their existence on this earth. Leading the way, clambering nimbly up the path is the man they nicknamed "the blond guy." He is their leader now. Their salvation depends on him. He has become more obliging, grabbing Emilia's suitcase despite her bland protests, and heaving it onto his shoulders to carry. In their brief pauses to catch their breath, he tries clumsily to distract Alessandro. After a few vain attempts, he asks him what he's thinking of doing in the future. "To be alive the day after tomorrow," the boy would like to answer, but of course he doesn't say it. He prefers to hide behind a vague "I don't know." The only thing that interests him now is to carry on as fast as possible up the mountain path without betraying his tiredness. His parents never once complain, nor ask for an additional break.

The air is growing colder, stinging their faces and hands. They have forgotten to bring gloves.

By the time they get to the high plateau, it is already dark. Saverio turns his torch on, but the beam is very narrow, and they can't find the wooden hut. Suddenly they hit upon it squatting in a dip like a terrified animal cowering in its lair. The cabin is dark and hostile. It doesn't look from the outside as though anybody has ever stayed in it. The broken boards used as a door open on their first attempt. Inside, the embers in the fireplace are burning slowly. In one corner, hanging from a hook, a gas lamp gives out a mean flicker of light. From the back of the room, two figures emerge wrapped in cloaks, or blankets—it is hard to tell. They do not greet them. Saverio asks for something to eat, and one of the two, the shape looks like that of an old woman, shuffles away. She returns carrying a half-empty basket of chestnuts. The other, a man, fumbles as he puts them on the embers to roast. They come out burnt on the outside and raw inside. Alessandro tries to send a couple down, but his gullet is not collaborating. His parents don't notice.

From a nook in the corner they hear a rustling sound and then a brief, strangled moan. "Is there someone else here?" Saverio asks, suddenly tense. The cloaked man takes him aside and speaks to him in thick dialect. "There's a woman, one of your people. She slipped on a scree and broke her leg. They had to bring her here." *One of your people?* Saverio has always pretended not to know that he is smuggling Jews. But there is something more urgent to attend to.

Marc leaps up, followed by his wife and son. The woman is lying on a straw pallet, a threadbare blanket thrown over her, covering her head and body. She looks like a cloth bundle, a forgotten piece of luggage.

"Ma'am?" Marc shakes her, forcing her to turn to one side and lower the blanket so that he can see her, at least. "Are you alone? Why have you been abandoned here?" He then asks the most important question: what can they do to help her? Without thinking, Marc reveals their real name and where they have come from—information even their guide is not supposed to know. He does it because at that moment he is no longer an escapee but, rather, a member of civilized society obliged to betray his origins in order to encourage a woman he doesn't even know, who nonetheless shares his destiny, to accept his help.

The woman, pale-faced with small features and perfectly tidy hair, perhaps from force of habit of good manners, answers, "I'm from Turin." She has no intention of giving them either her name or her story.

"I don't need anything; it's all taken care of," she adds after a pause. Emilia recognizes the snooty tone, so typical of upper-middle-class Piedmont Jews.

There's something unsettling and murky about her story, and the "Ferraris"—or whatever in hell they are called now—will not give up until they find out what is going on. Saverio sees their determination and decides to tell them himself. The woman was not alone. Her husband and two sons were with her. After her fall, she was the one that insisted they carry on and cross the border into Switzerland. The smuggler left her in a field. The border was quite close. He helped the men cross and then came back to get her. That's all there is to it. Of course, the smuggler received extra money from the husband and more is on its way from some relatives in Venice, who are not even Jewish. They're well-off, and they're organizing a new crossing, in the opposite direction, with a doctor, too, they promised.

There is absolute silence in the hut. The woman won't look at them. Alessandro can't control his outburst and stammers, "Your husband and sons left you in a field with a broken leg?" The room almost shudders with the horror that has been evoked. Emilia stares at her son fearfully.

"What do you know about anything?" The woman's composure has crumbled. "I was the one that insisted they went!" she wails. Her words now come out in a rush, stumbling over one another, as if each word were desperate to hijack the last. Her husband is not only Jewish, he's also one of the leaders of the anti-Fascist resistance group, Justice and Freedom. A photograph, *his photograph*, is circulating everywhere. Her boys are old enough for active duty, anybody could pick them up. This cursed passage to Switzerland is their only chance of salvation.

"But not for you!" Alessandro insists. He can't help himself. "How could they have accepted a wicked proposal like that?" The word "wicked" slips out unbidden, and he is mortified; words seem to have a life of their own sometimes. The woman has drawn herself up onto her elbows, almost into a sitting position. At least, that's what it looks like.

"I picked up a stick from the ground and yelled that if they didn't carry on, I'd break the other leg with it," she tells them. "They know me. They knew I would do it." She drops back onto the pallet. "They'll come and get me," she murmurs under the blanket.

Alessandro feels like he's drowning and can't remember how to get his head above water. He gasps for breath. He's surrounded by chaos and nothing else.

This woman saved her sons, and now she's fighting tooth and nail to make sure they are not judged unfairly.

Would his mother smash a leg in to save him? Yes, he thinks. She would.

This is where his thoughts come to a halt. The sense of the impenetrability of human actions is drowning him. God, too, is offended if you try to understand too much. Rabbi Bonfiglioli once read something in class: "You who can't see the twists of your own breath." He hadn't understood it at the time, but it came to mind at that moment.

CHAPTER 41

S till dark. They gather outside the hut, holding their bags. Saverio was the one to shake them awake from their fragile sleep—huddled under coats with their hats pulled down over their eyes, all three on a makeshift mattress stuffed with corn husks that creaked every time they moved. The cabin is quiet again. The two old people are nowhere to be seen. They may have left. The woman might be holding her breath in the hope that the strangers forget all about her. They start walking slowly. The residue of unconsumed sleep trammels their movements. The incline is steeper, and it is still pitch-black outside. Saverio turns the torch on for a second, switching it off again almost immediately to save the battery.

Their eyes must have become accustomed to the night. Alessandro manages to distinguish the shapes of things in the dark. They can all see their guide's hand pointing upwards. His wrist moves, and he points at something with a finger. There, at the end of the path, across a field on top of a plateau, finally, there is the border wire. *Their* wire. Their feet fly.

Men yelling and dogs barking meld into one terrifying sound.

"Halt! You! Hands in the air!"

Emilia's bag, which Saverio was carrying for her, dropped like a piece of lead on the grass.

It's strange, Alessandro manages to think in the flashing light that perhaps signals the end, how he has always thought that fear was a sensation linked to the psyche, like pain or love. Not something that attacks you physically in such a brutal fashion. His blood has congealed into a single block of ice, his eyes struggle to make sense of the intermittent green flashes, his mouth feels as though he's chewing iron. Icy metal is the barrel of the gun that the Fascist soldier, wolfdog on a leash scratching to be free, is pointing at his temple. They keep their hands in the air, terrified. Emilia, whose lips are ashen in a stark, white face, has wrapped her arms around her belly, as if she were protecting an imaginary child.

Saverio dares to take a few steps forward. One hand is still raised, as a sign of surrender, the other is outstretched, as a faltering request to open a dialogue. The soldier takes one leap and grabs Saverio by the collar of his jacket and starts shaking him violently.

"You! You! You shouldn't have done this to me! You should never have done this to me!" he yells, like a man possessed, waving the gun he had been holding against Alessandro's temple over his head.

What does he mean? Do they know each other? Their fear gives way to a devastating feeling of impotence. They are sinking, sinking into the quicksand of human misery.

Saverio has managed to free himself from the soldier's grasp. They are now facing each other, talking. Neither of them is yelling. They can't hear what they're saying.

Their guide returns to the group, distraught. "I've convinced him, but he wants money," he pants. "How much can you give him?" In a frenzy, Marc grips onto the figures as if they were a table of mental salvation. He counts the numbers out in his head, and counts them again, trying to remember what they had left. "Would ten or fifteen thousand be enough? he hazards. They need to keep something back for when they get to the "other side."

Saverio makes the offer. The Fascist is still brandishing the gun, but he's no longer pointing it at any of them. Alessandro has flopped onto the grass halfway between them, looking at everyone in the party but seeing no one. He hears the discussion becoming heated again, turning angry, but he doesn't care. The guide has returned to "their side" again. "I had to start again. I've convinced him, once more," he says, "but he wants the whole lot. Twenty-five thousand, not one lira less. His voice has become sharp, brutal.

"It's everything I own," Marc gasps. How did the Fascist soldier know? How did Saverio know? He staggers, having lost every point of reference.

Emilia is shouting, "Give it to him! Give it to him!"

Marc hesitantly pulls out an envelope from his inside jacket pocket. The ivory-colored letter paper looks like it comes from another planet and has unexpectedly landed in this world. Saverio grabs it out of Marc's hand and runs. The soldier counts the money and doesn't say a word. He calls the dog to heel with a whistle and in no time at all he is far away. The dog skips in front of his master, and they can hear it barking in the distance at the chorus of birds celebrating dawn.

They are all sitting on the grass; they are disoriented, done in. Each of them feels an obscure sense of shame for something they have seen in the others, or—worse—in themselves. Saverio keeps his eyes down.

"If you don't cross the border now, we'll bump into the patrol guards," he murmurs. They get up. Marc starts to dig around mechanically in his pockets to see whether there is any loose change there, but then he stops himself.

There are only a few steps to the wire fence, held up by a series of wooden stakes placed with maniacal precision at regular intervals. The smuggler lifts one that is not dug in properly, just resting on the ground.

"Slide underneath, hurry!"

Alessandro is the last to slip through. Saverio hands all the bags under the wire, and the wooden stake regains its upright position, presiding over the border undaunted.

A minute later and the blond smuggler's jacket is already swaying in the distance. It's almost morning, the birds have stopped singing.

As they walk on, their eyes start to regain their sight. The Swiss mountains are identical to the Italian ones. The sun is slowly painting them with color.

CHAPTER 42

H alt! *Chi siete?*" A German accent.
A trap.
This is not Switzerland.

Emilia's legs buckle and she drops to her knees.

The soldiers are wearing helmets and carrying rifles. There is a little white cross on the collar of their uniforms. They're German Swiss, Marc explains in a whisper. Emilia doesn't understand. Not only have her legs given way, her ears, too, are not functioning properly. What? Can't he hear they're speaking in Italian? Her husband tries to make her smile. It's true, this is Italian Switzerland, but the duty guards come from other cantons in the confederacy.

Alessandro understood right away. We're in Switzerland, he thinks. They can speak in whatever accent they like; he doesn't care.

His father is explaining to the soldiers that they are a Jewish family escaping from the Germans. He seems confident that those few words are enough.

"Come with us," the younger guard with brown hair and eyes says. He doesn't look German at all. He didn't even hear the escapee's explanation; his only task is to take them to the command post.

They are led down a footpath, the three of them sandwiched by the guards, one in front and one behind. Escorted in this way, their posture and gait instantly transform them into refugees.

The command post halfway down the mountain has nothing military about it. It looks like one of those mountain huts made of stone and wood, with curtains in the windows and window boxes full of flowers. The inside presents a stark contrast to the facade, however. There are two benches along the walls and an unassuming old desk behind which a noncommissioned officer is sitting. In Italy, he may have been a corporal. He asks for their papers without even looking up. The guards who brought the group stare into space. It is a ritual they take part in several times a day that holds no interest for them.

"Ferrari?" The officer waves the papers in his hand. "That's not a Jewish last name!" They're false identity papers, Marc hastily explains. Their real name is Rimon, which means "pomegranate" in Hebrew, one of the silver ornaments on the scroll of the Torah. He is a diamond cutter who lived in Holland before moving to Italy, but in actual fact he is British. His passport has been deposited for safe-keeping with the Swiss Legation in Genoa. He stops in his tracks. All these words are creating confusion, it's because someone has just pointed a gun at his son's temple and he has been so blind and so stupid, he didn't want to take out all the money he had in his pocket but all that's irrelevant now, it's not the time to confess, his life has always been so complicated but his explanation to the corporal *must not* be. He needs to come up with something essential, something that summarizes everything else. "The Germans are hunting us down," he says finally, and even that is too generic, ultimately not precise enough. Marc opens his arms in a gesture of defeat.

The officer appears not to have been listening. He continues to inspect the three identity cards that Alessandro had, a month ago now, manhandled in order to age them more quickly. He scrutinizes every stamp, lifts the documents up to the light as if they were counterfeit money. He gets up, runs to the room next door and returns a second later. He's middle-aged but he is still spry.

"These are not false papers. They come from an official administrative office," he states firmly.

"They may well be," Marc says, raising his voice. "We paid to get them. But those are not our names. The names are false, not the documents."

"You don't need false names to come to Switzerland," the officer spells out, proud of himself. He looks over at the guards, who are still at the door. The two young men nod. It's their job, but they, too, share with their officer a pure sentiment of national pride.

The guards. I've gotten it all wrong, I wasted words when they were not needed, I can try again with the guards, after all, they are the ones who saved us, who picked us up at the border. Marc grabs on to the arm of the younger guard who had said "come with us."

"We had to get false identities to cross Italy, which is occupied by the Germans. Don't you see?" he pleaded desperately.

"You said you were British, then that you were Jewish. Who's going to confirm any of it?" So, he was listening, even though he looked blank. "Our orders are to welcome only soldiers in uniform and people who can actually prove they are in danger. Switzerland can't just open the flood gates to everyone," he added, looking into the distance as if he were reciting the regulations off by heart, like a bored student being questioned at school.

Perhaps something softens inside him as he adds, with a hint of bitterness he is not aware of, "We can't take in others, even if we wanted to."

Marc intuits the change and looks again at the man in charge: "You have to believe me," he says softly. He can't seem to find any other words.

From his sudden embarrassment it is clear that the corporal has understood what the distinguished gentleman is clumsily insinuating. He stops him with his hand. "Circumcision on its own is not proof. It's a common practice even among those who are not Jewish." He picks up the papers again, perhaps to lend something tangible to his arguments. "I'll go and talk to the officer in command," he announces, scuttling out of the room and up the stairs.

They can hear the guards chatting quietly. One of them smiles suddenly; perhaps he's boasting to his mate about his prowess while he was on leave. The corporal beckons to Marc, "The commanding officer wants to speak to you," he says. Marc goes upstairs.

They can't hear anything from below. A uniform silence envelops the whole hut out there in the middle of nowhere. Then, suddenly, a man weeping.

Alessandro leaps to his feet. It's his father sobbing uncontrollably. He's never, ever heard his father cry. Everything is going to pieces. It's not like the icy grip of terror that paralyzes you when someone points a gun at your head: that is unadulterated terror, the fulminating sensation that for you the word "future" no longer exists. This is the total destruction of your past. The whole of your existence canceled out by a father's tears of surrender. There is a column that holds up your conception of what it is to be human. If that column crumbles, you no longer exist either.

He has come back downstairs. His face is devastated. He drops into a chair as far as possible away from them. Emilia is about to run over to him, but the corporal stops her. "Come upstairs, please. The commanding officer wants to speak to you, too." He climbs the stairs by her side.

Alessandro is left alone with his father. Not to approach him takes a supreme form of respect. Emilia soon returns, swaying as if she were dazzled by blinding light as she walks into the room. "He wants you now," she says under her breath. Alessandro doesn't realize at first that she is speaking to him.

The lieutenant seems kind, even though his gaze wanders around the room never quite looking directly at him. Clearly, the boy looks too young, even compared to the slightest of his soldiers. "What's your name?" he asks. The question everyone asks. Even the rabbi had opened with that move when they first met. Here there is an ulterior motive. In this situation, he is David and he has to vanquish Goliath. He almost shouts out his Biblical last name, Rimon.

The papers say "Ferrari," and there is no official stamp declaring that they belong to the "Jewish race." They are false papers that his father paid for. Yes, that's what his parents said, too. The commander looks a little impatient, as if it were not the lie that annoyed him but the repetition of the lie. They *told* you but I will help you *understand*. Alessandro feels an increasingly strong charge running through him. However, every answer he gives the commander receives the same monotonous comment: yes, you've already told me. His accent is slightly French. Alessandro wonders whether his ancestors were occupying forces under Napoleon.

"Excuse me," Alessandro says, unable to hold back any longer. "If you know everything, tell me this one thing. If we were not Jews being chased out of our country, why would we take all these risks, pay someone to smuggle us across the border, in mortal danger of being ambushed and robbed of the little savings we still had—as in fact happened? Why on earth would we have run a risk of this kind?"

Aroused from his torpor, the commanding officer says resentfully, "What do you think? Do you really believe people want to come here just because they're in danger? The whole of Europe would like to take refuge here. Far away from the war, from air raids and hunger, from . . . everything. Soldiers deserting the army and, yes, Jews and others who are persecuted, come through, but there are also hundreds and hundreds of low lives of all kinds, including those with political or personal scores to settle." He stops and looks at the boy. He notes again that he looks too young. "We can't take everybody in, you must see that," he insists, although his tone is no longer Napoleonic. "It would be an injustice to those who are really being persecuted, whose spaces would be filled." Alessandro understands. Harking back to an objective, generalized reality will be the end of them. The commanding officer is looking at him with a kind of pity in his eyes—that of a judge who is duty bound by Law to mete out Justice.

He sends for the parents, who arrive under the escort of the corporal. He starts to explain, looking at the corporal in search of support and confirmation. There is no need to be afraid. They will not be sent back into the maws of the Germans or the Fascists. They, like the smugglers, know the shifts of the border patrol well. They will take care to send them back to "the other side" safely, when there are no patrols.

What will we do on the other side? "We don't even have the money to take a tram!" Marc yells.

Alessandro is silent. He feels the shock waves of an uncontrollable force surging within him. "You will not succeed. You will not have me." Then, in a perilously calm voice, he adds, "I'm not turning back," and lies down on the floor.

The boy has grabbed the leg of a sturdy, dark wooden table used as a desk; his hands tightly woven together. He will not let go; the commanding officer is sure of it. The man feels a sense of dejected uneasiness wash over him—the scene has disturbed him considerably. He looks over to his subordinate who, in his turn, gawps at him, eyes wide. The officer grabs the "illegal" by the feet and starts tugging, but he knows better than his commanding officer that when fingers are interlocked, the more you pull, the more they form an iron grip. He is sweating, and breaks off for a minute. He then calls out for the other soldiers. They run up the stairs, clutching their rifles, and come to a halt at the door. Now three of them are tugging, the youngest guard trying to loosen the boy's grip by lifting one of his fingers, but his hold seems destined to last for eternity.

You can pull as much as you like, with all your might, but you will not win. I am Samson. Rather, I am all the Samsons on Rabbi Bonfiglioli's inkwell. I represent nothing to you. You will save another who is "more worthy than me," you will claim. When I was a child, I would only eat rice when the moon was out. I know. It's not a particular feat. There is nothing extraordinary, or even significant, about it. It's just that I believe nobody else has ever decided to eat rice with the moon. I loved my aunt more than my mother. Maybe that's not even true, but it is my own labyrinth, and it can't be repeated. I always think that God must have an endless imagination. I don't understand how every human being has whorls on their fingertips that are different from every other person on the planet, even in the most far-flung of forgotten islands. This is why you can't exchange me even for a scientist who has discovered the secrets of the movements of the planets. I will resist in this place because the floor I am lying on is built on this earth where nobody can decide to make me, of all people, disappear.

The guards have stopped. They look at the corporal. "He's little more than a boy," they say. The corporal looks at the commanding officer. The man sighs, without saying a word. Then he bends down under the table and says, "Come out of there. I promise, we'll start over and examine your case properly."

Alessandro lets go but stays sitting on the ground, in a residual quest for safety, perhaps.

The commanding officer turns his gaze to the parents. It is

with them that he would like to start the negotiation. Okay, he is now convinced that they are indeed Jews, but he can't just follow his gut instincts, there is a chain of command to follow, tangible evidence must be produced, a state of mind is not sufficient.

"My British passport is deposited in your Legation in Genoa. Send for it!" Marc has leaped to his feet, a new light shining in his eyes.

"Do you really think we have time for that sort of thing?" The lieutenant's expression is bitter, disheartened. He meant immediate, real evidence—an old document hidden at the bottom of a suitcase, for example, or a school copy book with the boy's real surname on it.

It is the boy who now jumps up. He has taken off his coat and jacket, his eyes aflame. He looks crazy, shouting, "Give me some scissors!" The commanding officer is suspicious. The boy isn't going to threaten to commit suicide, is he? But it is the mother who grabs the scissors on the desk and is now sitting back in her chair, the worn-out jacket she picked up from the ground in her lap, calmly unpicking the sleeve seam. She stops. The scissors brandished mid-air look like the sword of an avenging angel. The son rushes to her side and then lifts *the thing* up victoriously: the gold chain and pendant that Nonna Rachele had left him.

The Star of David carved in relief on the pendant continues to gleam even in these foreign lands, undaunted.

"Put a call through to Chiasso," the commanding officer orders. "Tell them we're sending along three more."

CHAPTER 43

Perhaps this is what life is, a stupid little ditty that suddenly, of its own accord, rings out like a recoil in the most solemn moments of your existence.

The commanding officer tells the corporal, "Write their name clearly," and smiles as if he were in a social setting, before adding, "Their real ones, of course." Again, as if he were the host of a party saying goodbye to his favorite house guests and worrying about where they should go next, he starts explaining. The place is called Sagno, and, well, Sagno is not that close to Chiasso. "How are you planning to get there?" he asks politely.

The three of them are a little disconcerted. They've only been in Switzerland a few hours, and they had not exactly been planning to be tourists.

"Do you have any money?" he continued. "The best solution would be a taxi."

Going to a refugee camp in a taxi. Some prankster angel must be laughing. "The trip should cost around a hundred lire," the commanding officer and the colonel agree. Marc searches his pockets and finds a few coins; he collects the rest from Emilia's bag. The commanding officer is visibly relieved and goes on to provide some practical tips. Near Chiasso, there's a processing center where they are expected. It's called Lazzaretto. He knows the name of the place doesn't bode well but there's nothing to worry about, it's not a hospital. It's an ancient building that's been there for centuries. He nods to the corporal, "You take them," he says. It's not clear who'll pay his return fare.

Emilia notices the nod; she feels perhaps that some kind of agreement has been made between the two men. The whole thing may be an invention: a further trap. She starts trembling again.

The taxi descends into the valley slowly. They are in the outskirts of Chiasso and, to the left, suddenly, they see the parallel posts marking the border. The Swiss and Italian flags flap in the wind; every now and then they even touch one another. "I knew it: it's a trick! They're taking us back to Italy," Emilia gasps, a tableau of fear.

Alessandro looks at her. "Don't worry," he says.

It looks as though the taxi is getting closer and closer to the border. On the Italian side, they can clearly see two armed German soldiers standing next to the Fascist guard. A splinter of terror pierces the inside of the car like a bolt of lightning. It is only for a fraction of a second. The taxi drives right past.

"They called from Sagno." Marc was walking in front of the corporal. "They've sent over our details."

"Very well." The guard at Lazzaretto looked bored. "Sign here: name, last name, date and place of birth, address in Italy," he recites, holding out a big ledger, like the ones they use to register visitors at an art exhibition. The corporal has vanished; he slipped away while they were focused on writing down their details.

They have to wait for a medical checkup and all the other formalities. In this place, too, there are benches along the walls but nobody sitting on them. In the distance, they can see a few people, sitting on old chairs here and there. Near a window, a clutch of people stands close together. Are they arguing? No, they're praying: it's Friday evening. They hadn't realized; counting minutes had taken over their days. They lean towards the group, listening.

Suddenly they hear the strains of the *Lekhah Dodi*, "Let's go, my beloved, to meet the bride, and let us welcome the presence of the Shabbat." For centuries someone has been singing these words.

The Sabbath has come in.

There are not many of them. Certainly not enough to reach the quorum required by the *minyan*.

Alessandro makes a move to join them; his mother follows.

The document on the facing page is the original acceptance form from the Swiss Customs Office filled in by my husband, Luciano Tas. This novel is inspired by him and his story. All his life, Luciano held a deep-seated sense of gratitude towards Switzerland.

We are grateful to the State Archive of the Canton Ticino at Bellinzona (Switzerland) for granting permission to reproduce the document held in their Internments Collection for the years 1943–45.

DICHIARAZIONE DI STATO CIVILE

da trasmettere al Comando di Gendarmeria col rapporto. Controllare tutte le indicazioni sulla scorta
dei documenti personali. La dichiarazione deve essere scritta di pugno dal dichiarante.

PERMESSO DI DIMORA - SOGGIORNO - DOMICILIO N. _____ *Ebreo*

| Cognome
Familienname
Nom | *Cas* | Nome
Vorname
Prénom | *Luciano Filippo* |

Padre / Vater / Père *di Jacques* Madre / Mutter / Mère *di Giuseppina Cas*

nato a / geboren zu / né à _*Genova*_ (_____) il / den / le *4 febbraio 1927*

originario di / Heimatberechtigt in / originaire de _*Londra*_ (_____)

dimorante a / Wohnhaft in / domicilié à *Isola del Cantone (Genova)* via / Strasse / rue *Pontevecchio 2*

professione / Beruf / profession _*studente*_

celibe / ledig / célibataire ammogliato con / verheiratet mit / marié avec *celibe*

Incorporazione militare / Militäreinteilung / Incorporation militaire *Con i genitori: Si riferisce alle loro dichiarazioni*

_____

Data: *15/10/43*

Firma del dichiarante:

Luciano Cas

43 1091 5000

About the Author

Lia Levi is the author of many books for children and adults. She has been awarded the Elsa Morante First Novel Prize (1994), the Castello Prize for Fiction (1994), the Moravia Prize (2001), and the Strega Youth Prize (2018). She lives in Rome.